perfect pitch

perfect pitch

2) foreign field

EDITED BY
SIMON KUPER

review

First published in softback in 1998
by HEADLINE BOOK PUBLISHING

A REVIEW softback

10 9 8 7 6 5 4 3 2 1

ISBN 0 7472 7697 8

Typeset by
Letterpart Limited, Reigate, Surrey
Printed and bound in Great Britain by
Mackays of Chatham PLC, Chatham, Kent

HEADLINE BOOK PUBLISHING
A division of Hodder Headline PLC
338 Euston Road
London NW1 3BH

contents

acknowledgements

Thanks to Richard Adams, Peter Aspden, Gary Blumberg, Sophie Breese, Tom Butler, Tomaso Capuano, Robert Chote, Maria Amélia Dalsenter, Patrick Lewers, Simon Luke, Annalena McAfee, Fiona McMorrough, Matthijs van Nieuwkerk, Simon Pennington, Vivienne Schuster, Timon Smith, Henk Spaan, Michael Thompson-Noel, Leo Verheul and David Winner, and to Ian Marshall and his colleagues at Headline.

Submissions to *Perfect Pitch* are welcome. These should be accompanied by a stamped, self-addressed envelope and sent to: The Editors, Perfect Pitch, c/o Headline Book Publishing, 338 Euston Road, London, NW1 3BH.

introduction

Four years ago, when a teenage Brazilian forward joined PSV Eindhoven, the Dutch journalist Frans Oosterwijk decided to write a short book about him. Frans spent a season with the boy, and in June 1995 the Dutch literary football magazine *Hard Gras* devoted an entire issue to the result. It was called *Ronaldo Comes From Rio*.

Frans is a suave inhabitant of Amsterdam; Ronaldo was a naïf from Rio. They were made for each other. Later Frans followed the boy to Barcelona and Paris, updating his account for this second issue of *Perfect Pitch*.

'Aha!' you may say. 'So that is why you have called the issue "Foreign Field". Your writers write about foreign countries!'

There is something in that. The geographical range runs from Porto Alegre to Cardiff. Gary Lineker is discovered in Argentina. And of course our debut issue was called 'Home Ground'.

But, as you would expect from a publication as highbrow as this one, the 'Foreign Field' theme has another meaning too. Each writer writes with love, but also with a certain distance to subject. Blake Morrison, man of letters, reads footballers' autobiographies. Simon Inglis, the football grounds man, tries children. Harry Ritchie, a Scot, stands back to take a long hard look. Lynne Truss reveals the future, another pretty foreign field.

'All very clever you might think,' to quote Stuart Ford,

another of our authors, 'but who cares?' Well, there is a certain tendency in British football literature to write about home – about the club you support. I mentioned in issue one that *Perfect Pitch* would not print anything along the lines of 'I stood on the terraces at Hartlepool for years and we always lost and it rained'. Strangely enough, 98 per cent of the submissions we received were along exactly those lines. Most of them were funny and well written. Someone should set up another magazine to print them.

Simon Kuper, editor

wright and wright again: a grandstand view of football memoirs

BLAKE MORRISON

In the league table of literary forms, the football memoir comes near the bottom. Heading the premiership are poetry and fiction; 'general' autobiography, as written by politicians or public figures, ranks somewhere in the middle; but the soccer memoir is down there in the low reaches, along with gardening, fishing and cricket. Or even lower: cricket being a slow and strategic game, cricketers are imagined to be contemplative – unlike footballers who are thought not to have a thought in their heads. If there were a non-league their literary offerings could be relegated to, that is where critics would put them.

There have been some good books about football by footballers – Eamon Dunphy and Garry Nelson come to mind. And in a world where players can enhance their careers through mastery of the television soundbite, the idea that footballers are unavoidably inarticulate looks not only snobbish but out of date. Still, there remains a suspicion that most football autobiographies aren't truly autobiographical – that someone else has done the work of getting the words down on the page. Some memoirs acknowledge the role of a ghost or scribe, though publishers naturally prefer to play it down, since the 'with' word (as in 'by Frank Striker, with Willie Hack') is such a turn-off. The paperback of *Jack Charlton: The Autobiography** makes no mention of a significant other on its cover, but in the acknowledgements Big

* published by Corgi, £5.99

9

Jack pays tribute to the 'co-operation' of Peter Byrne, 'who supped me with in recording many happy and some not-so-happy moments'. We infer from this that Byrne didn't put words in his subject's mouth, but transcribed or taped words he'd actually said, sober or otherwise, then edited them down. It's a time-honoured process, and skilfully done (as Byrne does it), it can result in a powerful read. But it does make the question of authorship a difficult one. Where no help is acknowledged at all, as in Ian Wright's autobiography*, the worries only increase. Is Wright hiding someone, or did he really do the business himself? The latter is, if anything, the more troubling possibility. Football is its own language: fluency in a second language – including the language of tactics or technical analysis – is meant to be for managers, coaches or commentators, not for players, or not for famous players at the height of their career. Ian Wright is exceptional in having produced his autobiography while in his prime. But at least he was over thirty when he wrote it. Few would expect David Beckham or Steve McManaman to produce a classic memoir in the wake of this year's World Cup. Memoirs are for the twilight years.

Publishers take a different line, of course. They may not know much about football, but they will pay good money to entice a sexy young player to come up with a 'controversial' book (i.e., one in which the player grasses on his mates). If they haven't been already, Beckham and McManaman will certainly be invited to produce memoirs if England have a good run in France. The stuff of the successful young Nineties footballer – Armani suits, sponsorship deals, liaisons with Spice Girls – makes dully familiar reading, but this could be overlooked if we had the Goal that Won the Final to enjoy, or were told what it's like to take the trophy on a lap of honour. British football still

* *Mr Wright* (Collins Willow, £5.99)

lives in the shadow of 1966. Even the Keegans and Dalglishes, who as players enjoyed club success in Europe (and have interesting tales to tell as managers), don't know what it's like to play in a World Cup final. Big Jack has one over on them here. He devotes a whole chapter to 30 July 1966, which looks modest alongside David Thompson's full-length book *4-2* but finds room not only for a description of each goal but for quirkier items – like the difficulty he had walking down from the Royal Box on studs; or the urine sample he had to give after the match (he'd been randomly tested so many times before, the doctors honoured the occasion by presenting him with a plastic hat inscribed 'For one who gave his best for England – the Jimmy Riddle Trophy'); or the night of partying, which ended with him crashing out on the sofa of a man called Lenny he'd never met before, somewhere in Leytonstone; or the trip back up the A1 next day, which included a stop-off at a transport cafe for egg and chips, 'the best meal I'd had for weeks'. Here is the authentic, personal, unofficial voice of history, much more interesting to hear than tales of posh noshes and triumphant waves from an open-top coach.

The best football memoirs have important stories to relate: the other Charlton, Bobby, had the Munich air disaster to bear witness to as well. But they must also tell their story in a way that hasn't been told a million times before. This is difficult for modern footballers, who – public property in magazines and on websites from an early age – will have had their story told a thousand times before it reaches book form. In one respect, the memoirists of 1966 were equally disadvantaged since, like their Nineties heirs, they lived in the age of television, and when they came to relive famous moments were inhibited by the knowledge that the camera had already been there before. Billy Wright and Tommy Lawton had no such problem: most of the games they describe were seen only by those in the crowd that day, and their accounts feel fresh, not mere action replays in words.

In *Football Ambassador* (1945)° Eddie Hapgood had even more to offer, telling remarkable stories of the intersection of football and politics in the late 1930s and early 1940s. In 1938, Hapgood captained England against Germany in Berlin. The German team, a 'bunch of arrogant, sun-bronzed giants', had been chosen 'with as much thoroughness as if it was destined to be Hitler's personal bodyguard'. A crowd of 110,000 came to roar them on in front of Goering and von Ribbentrop. Before kick-off, at the behest of Stanley Rous of the FA and Sir Nevile Henderson, the British ambassador, the English team had to give the Nazi salute. There was no appeasement in the scoreline, though: England won 6-3. Hapgood tells the tale well, with unabashed patriotic fervour. There's a similar tone to his story of 'the battle of Highbury', against the Italians, in 1934. England won this 3-2, though not without injury, including the broken nose Hapgood suffered himself, which he came round from in the dressing room before returning to the field bandaged up:

> The Italians had gone berserk, and were kicking every-body and everything in sight. My injury had apparently started the fracas, and, although our lads were trying to keep their tempers, it's a bit hard to play like a gentle-man when somebody closely resembling an enthusiastic member of the Mafia is wiping his studs down your legs, or kicking you up in the air from behind . . . One of the newspaper men was so disgusted with the display that he signed his story 'By Our War Correspondent' . . . I thought then that I never wanted to see an Italian again in my life . . . The probable reason for the display of the Italians was that they were under a terrific inducement

° published by Sporting Handbooks, 9s 6d.

from Mussolini. Each man had been promised that if they won, he would get a substantial money award of something like £150, an Alfa-Romeo car, and what was more important to them, exemption from their annual military service.

The year before, in Rome, Hapgood cleared the ball into the crowd, where, allegedly, it hit Mussolini 'just above his lunch' ('I often wish it had been something more lethal than a football'). In May 1939, in Milan, Hapgood had another go at Mussolini: with enthusiastic fans clamouring outside the England team hotel, he 'stepped out on the balcony and gave the crowd a quick flip of my arm, the nearest I could get to a Fascist salute'. This doesn't seem very ambassadorial, but he and his team, touring Europe as war loomed, were often praised as 'ambassadors'. Hapgood also tells the story of turning out for Arsenal against Spurs during the war while officially being confined to barracks for an offence: two RAF officers escorted him from the airfield to the White Hart Lane dressing room and even walked with him down the players' tunnel. It's hard to compete with stuff like this, which has the feel of history as well as sport (in recent decades, only the Hillsborough and Heysel disasters seem momentous in that way). Nor would footballers now think of bothering to describe in loving, guidebook detail the foreign parts they've visited. Both Hapgood and Billy Wright could do so knowing their readers were unlikely to have ventured abroad except for war service, and would find such travel notes exotic.

Part of the charm of a memoir like Hapgood's is simply nostalgia. You learn things you'd forgotten or hadn't thought about – the fact that teams used to travel to away games on public trains, for example – and you're brought up against values which have disappeared not just from football but from life. Here's Hapgood on playing in front of George VI at Wembley, and uttering sentiments it would be impossible to imagine even from Bobby Moore: 'It makes a great deal of difference when one of the Royal Family is up there in the Box. Everybody seems to try and play a little better. And there's often much less stoppage for infringements.' At moments like this, the gulf between old-style footballing memoirs and modern-day ones looks vast. 'I started my football at Old Trafford and that is where I intend to finish it,' wrote Bobby Charlton in *My Soccer Life* (1964)*; and so he did. 'In all my twenty-one years at Molineux I never had a single row with Stan Cullis [the manager],' said Billy Wright in *One Hundred Caps and All That* (1962)†. Both books belong to an era when being taken on as an apprentice to scrub the boots of older players was considered an incomparable blessing, when you deferred to the manager and yes-sired the chairman, when it wasn't uncommon to stay with one club for your whole career, when it was customary – the war not far behind – to rail against dirty foreigners (Germans and Italians especially), and when being English was thought a mark of superiority – for wasn't it us that had given the world the game, and wasn't ours the tough, open, naturally attacking game which other nations could stifle only by dour defence or foul play?

Despite the huge differences between football autobiographies then and now, there are certain constants in the genre. Typically, the player will begin with his humble origins: Jack Charlton recalls an outside toilet and sleeping four to a bed with his brothers, while Ian Wright mentions his mother's struggles to keep her four kids in decent clothes. Tribute will be paid to a teacher or sage who steered the headstrong boy along the right path, and to the talent scout or manager who first recognised his footballing potential: the Men to Whom He Owes Everything

* published by Sportsman's Book Club, no price given
† published by Robert Hale, 15s.

(Or At Any Rate A Lot). Then we'll hear about initiation rites: the trial, the invitation to sign on, the first game with the reserves, the bruising clash with a jealous older player from the same club, the first-team debut, the first goal, the first serious injury or loss of form, the first national cap . . . Later chapters in the book will be more bitty. One chapter is always devoted to compiling a dream team – the Eddie Hapgood Best-Ever Team, Billy Wright's 'You Should Have Seen . . .' list, the Gary McAllister All-Star Select. Another chapter will open the door a little on the player's home life, the adoring wife and adored kids. Another will tell you how he relaxes – by playing golf, invariably, though Ian Wright also plays the saxophone. Yet another will condemn the prying sensationalism of the media, with exception made for a handful of honourable 'gentlemen of the press' (from whose ranks, of course, the book's ghostwriter will have come). At regular intervals, as if conscious that the talk of fame and riches may be giving the wrong idea, the player will solemnly remind us why he plays the game: 'It's a matter of pride. The day I step on to the field working out my pay packet, that's the day I will pack up' (Bobby Charlton); 'It's about pride and about doing the right thing every step of the way . . . Players should always remember the debt that they owe the fans' (Ian Wright); 'I don't do it for the money. I do it because I genuinely enjoy it' (Gary McAllister). There'll be some dressing-room gossip, but nothing dangerous or outright malicious. Most important of all, the book will give us goals.

How much the genre has changed in some ways, and how little in others, can be seen by comparing the autobiographies of the two Mr Wrights: Billy (twenty-two seasons with Wolves before, during and after the Second World War) and Ian (Crystal Palace and Arsenal). Billy Wright's book is prefaced with a quote from A.E. Housman – 'That is the land of lost content/I see it shining plain'. Eric Cantona aside, footballers don't often quote poetry, but this strikes the right elegiac note, since the book begins with Wright's sudden retirement from football at thirty-five. Having begun at the end, he then takes us back to his boyhood – his father was an iron foundry worker in the Black Country – and to his arrival on the ground staff at Wolves, on a wage of £2 a week, at the age of fourteen. In those days, Manchester United weren't the only club with a vigorous youth scheme, and the boss of Wolves, Major Buckley, who wore horn-rimmed specs and plus-fours, was always on the lookout for new talent. His only worry about Wright was his slight build, but when he told him, after six months, he'd have to let him go the boy burst into tears and was reprieved. The rest is history and winners' medals: club captain at 23, captain of England at 24; one FA Cup win and three league champion-ships; 105 international caps between 1946 and 1959. Until he was in his thirties, Wright had no time for romance or marriage, because of his dedication to the game. But at 34 he was surprised by Joy – one of the three singing Beverley Sisters. A daughter followed, then a CBE, then a trip to the home of the then Home Secretary R.A. Butler. Rab spoke of the wisdom of chaps getting out while still at the top. His words came back a few weeks later, as Billy struggled with the six-mile runs that were an essential part of training in those days. He'd already lasted three seasons more than he might have by switching positions from wing-half to centre-half. Now he was knackered. It was time to pack it in.

His career ends here, but his book doesn't: more than half of it consists of analysis and advice. His criticisms of the short passing game, and of wingers, look odd now, but not without substance, and many of his predictions of how the game could and should develop have since been fulfilled: a smaller premier league; grounds with a family atmosphere where everyone is under cover and can sit down; more television coverage; the use of substitutes. It is a sober book, and all highly proper, but in the last sentence Billy Wright takes a huge risk and uses the word 'darned'.

Ian Wright's tongue is somewhat sharper. He started f***ing (his asterisks) at team-mates while playing football at school, and went on from there, though he defends his language as 'just the usual sort of industrial banter that takes place in any office or factory'. Wright defends, or else denies, quite a lot in *Mr Wright* – spitting, abuse of referees, violence against other players. Self-righteousness is embedded even in the title: I may not be right, mister, but I'm never wrong. Still, Ian Wright has good reason for wanting to rebut the many things he has been accused of over the years, and, for all its defensiveness, his book is very engaging. It endears itself partly because the author knows he's been lucky, can remember what it was like having to get up at six o'clock in the morning to go to work in a place with cold, ankle-deep water and stinking chemicals. A cheeky South Londoner, he drifted from school into a spell of petty offending, for which he finally received a jail sentence. He spent only five days behind bars, but it was a Road to Damascus experience: thereafter he resolved to do better, not least with the all-black Sunday morning side he played for, Ten Em Bee. He had to wait till he was twenty-one for the chance to turn professional – an extraordinarily late start, though he was quick off the mark in other respects, having by this time fathered three sons by three different women. A partnership with Mark Bright at Palace, and marriage to the loyal Debbie, settled him down. He's still a bit flash and hotheaded on the field, but he can't, he says, be anything else: it's all part of being fired up.

The Wrights have very different temperaments. Conscious of his status as a football ambassador, Billy doesn't dare be irreverent: he remains highly discreet, and is pious in praise of Walter Winterbottom and his 4-2-4 system. Ian Wright, in the more intimate 1990s, is free both to be witty – one frightening defender is described as being 'about twenty feet tall with muscles on his breath' – and to be acid about those he has clashed with, or who haven't picked him, notably Graham Taylor, whose droning, incomprehensible team talks he sends up something rotten. Ian also lays into Terry Venables for failing to give him a regular England place. But then it's easy to slag off a former manager. When speaking about his current bosses, Arsene Wenger and Glenn Hoddle, Wright observes the convention of politeness. What he really thinks of them we won't know until they've been replaced or Wright is no longer in contention for a place in their sides.

Ian Wright isn't short on self-belief, but he hasn't the same confidence about national prospects as Billy had in 1962, when imperial swagger was the norm. The fact that England had never won the World Cup, the humiliations against the United States in 1950 and Hungary (twice) in 1953 and 1954, the wretched South American tour of 1959 (0-2 against Brazil, 1-4 against Peru, 1-2 against Mexico): none of this seemed to matter to Billy Wright, who could 'look forward to the time when England will beat the rest of the world – for, make no mistake, that time is coming'. Bobby Charlton, two years later, was more emphatic still: 'I think England will win the World Cup in 1966.' Except for the lack of home advantage, there's no reason to be less optimistic about the 1998 World Cup than we were about 1966. The modern tone, though, is worldlier and warier. 'There's a World Cup coming up with England and I dare not think about it,' says Ian Wright, cautiously, then adds, in a dreamy Roy-of-the-Rovers sort of way, as if from the subs' bench: 'How about coming on in the World Cup final and getting the winner?' Stranger things have happened. But neither Glenn Hoddle nor his players would dare sound so certain of success as Alf Ramsey, Bobby Moore, the Charlton brothers and Co. sounded in the build-up to 1966.

After the energy and abrasiveness of *Mr Wright, Captain's Log* (1995)° by Gary McAllister, captain of Coventry City and Scotland, is a mediocre performance. It's a memoir written in that jaunty exclamation-mark style which footballers, left to themselves, seem to favour ('the following Tuesday – two days later – I went to South Africa with United and that same day we moved house!'), and is short on insight and indiscretion. True, there are some pleasingly barbed remarks along the way, not least against Brian Clough (who tried but failed to sign McAllister from Leicester City) and Eric Cantona (whose part in Leeds United's championship he seeks to play down). But anyone looking for inside track on Scotland's chances in France will be disappointed: 'Scotland as a football nation remains an enigma,' McAllister tells us. 'We can beat the best and lose to the worst. Sometimes [the] picture is an X-certificate, other times it's a weepy, but it's always an adventure and occasionally it's even a spectacular! But it's never dull.' True, but we hardly need a book from Scotland's captain to tell us this when we could hear the same in any pub.

McAllister's book illustrates the essential problem of football memoirs. To be interesting, such books have to spill beans. But a player who still wants a future in football (as most players do even when they cease playing) has to mind his words. To publish and be damned is fine if you plan to emigrate or run a pub, but not if you want to keep in with the lads. What sounds reckless and hilarious in a brief after-dinner speech (and people like Tommy Docherty, Paddy Crerand and Geoff Hurst can do wicked turns on the speaking circuit) will usually be tame by the time it's been translated into book form. An honest book from a top player would be wonderful to have. An honest book from a top manager would be wonderful, too:

° published by Mainstream, £14.99

perhaps Hugh McIlvanney will tease something out of Alex Ferguson now that the Manchester United manager has been signed up to do his memoirs. But such honesty is hard to imagine. In the meantime we're better off with a book like Pete Davies's *All Played Out* – or with Eamon Dunphy and Garry Nelson.

If winning World Cup games has anything to do with a winning autobiographical persona, then Ian Wright and England will do better in France than Gary McAllister and Scotland. Finding the net and finding the right word aren't the same, though. Suppose Paul Gascoigne could turn a better phrase than John Updike – he'd still not have stretched the extra inch to turn in that golden chance against Germany in Euro 96. Or suppose Gordon Durie could write like Irvine Welsh – that wouldn't make it any easier to get past the Brazilian defence in France. In books, command of language is vital; in football, it counts for almost nothing. The only articulacy to be devoutly wished for from British players this summer is articulacy with the ball.

three lions on my shirt?

STUART FORD

My childhood footballing career before pulling on an England shirt can quite neatly be split into the times that were spent in crap teams and the times that weren't.

Crap teams had three important and defining characteristics: a crap kit, a crap name and, naturally, crap players. I spent many muddy weekend mornings in the Liverpool junior Sunday leagues playing for teams like 17th Fairfield A (named after a scout troop) and Gingerbread (true), usually in kits which in terms of style might once have been worn by Stockport County reserves. In the satin-dominated world of an Adidas-conscious eleven-year-old circa 1981 this was humiliating.

Crap teams spent most Sunday mornings being goaded, intimidated and ultimately crushed by teams that weren't crap. They weren't crap by virtue of their well-drilled squads of fast and tenacious scallywags (fifteen mini-Robbie Fowlers), their logo-adorned strips and their glamorous team names, like Ash Celtic and Roby Eagles. The names usually had origins in the pubs from the poorer and tougher districts of the city and an Under-12 side would be the most junior representatives of an Ajax-style academy of boys' and men's teams run from the same pub. A promising young player might spend twenty years working his way up through the ranks while his spitting, swearing and head-butting skills were lovingly nurtured within the academy. I would console myself that if you were a half-decent player in a crap team it was at least possible to stand out as a maverick and flamboyant talent.

As well as 17th Fairfield A and Gingerbread there was Leyfield, a team managed by my father, which partly explains my sentimentality towards crap teams. I always felt that Leyfield were worthy of more respect than most other crap teams by virtue of a name that could easily have been drawn from a pub, thereby conferring some much needed credibility. In truth, Leyfield was named after the main road nearest our house, but I always hoped that others would be duped. It dawned on me in later years that half the kids in the Under-12 league we played in were already regulars in the local pubs and unlikely to be fooled in this way.

Leyfield's first ever match epitomised the plight of a crap team. It was a midweek game against Dynamo Stoneycroft, a non-crap team named after the notorious Stoneycroft pub. They had a silky blue Adidas kit – very Ipswich Town circa Arnold Mühren – and by half-time we were 5–0 down. The evening light was fading badly and during the opening minutes of the second half the Leyfield players were growing slowly invisible. The blue-shirted Stoneycroft players should have been no easier to spot, but it seemed that the entire team was wearing the new Keegan Colt boots. These had a distinctive fluorescent green undersole so you could at least see both of the Stoneycroft player's feet as he came in from the side to tackle you.

Continued reckless intimidation and almost zero visibility led to an 8–0 scoreline with a full fifteen minutes to play. The margin would have been greater without Dave Egan, our bespectacled goliath of a centre back, who halted wave upon wave of Stoneycroft attacks with a series of bone-crunching tackles. When the myopic Dave landed one of those tackles on the referee the real drama began.

'You dirty fat f—. Get off the f— pitch!' screamed the ref as he writhed around on the ground trying to avoid the spitting from the Stoneycroft players.

'You can't send me off for a foul that wasn't on an opponent,' misquoted the cerebral young Dave from the 'You Are The Ref' page in *Shoot* magazine.

This seemed to have dumbfounded the ref until, from his temporary grass-level view, he noticed that Dave was wearing his brother's rugby boots which brandished metallic studs of a length that even quoting Clive Thomas couldn't excuse. Dave was told to leave the pitch or change his footwear. Unable to face the final period without our defensive rock, we swiftly persuaded little Jay Aitken, our substitute, to lend his boots to the centre back. Dave soldiered on to the finish (9–0) in a pair of Patrick-Keegan Colt that were two sizes too small.

I did jog over to the touchline with five minutes left and offered Jay my boots so he could come on for a bit.

'No thanks. I'm crap,' said Jay.

Confidence was already at a low.

As I mumbled and blushed a path through my early teens and developed a semblance of a footballing reputation, I found myself playing for better and better sides. Sides of the calibre of Trophy Pegasus which drew its ranks, except for me, entirely from the Huyton schools team (Huyton being a satellite town which made most of Liverpool look like Belgravia). They had to play in Liverpool because there was nobody left worth playing against in Huyton. I signed for them because of the munificent personal terms they offered – free shinpads, door-to-door chauffeuring and my name on the back of my shirt. Who could refuse?

Of course, I was often goaded about my posh school or my gross misunderstanding of street fashion. That was just from the management. It was never really a problem so long as I held my own on the pitch. Whatever the social gulf between me and those around me, there was a shared sense of enthusiasm and pride at the pace and skill of a team at its peak. In a city like Liverpool, every male is kicking a ball from the age of three. A crack team of fourteen-year-olds, before lack of opportunity, cynicism, women and other less pleasant distractions have taken a hold, can be a football purist's delight. Of course, the tendency is towards ball play and every good team would have seven or eight hugely skilful players. Trophy Pegasus were no different to the extent that when a slightly younger kid called McManaman played in a few pre-season friendlies for us, he wasn't even the best dribbler in the side. In those days he tended to rely on outright speed. As I learned in later years, it's that single quality which allows a McManaman or a Hignett (a regular former opponent who last season partnered Juninho in Middles-brough's midfield) to go on and make it when the other ten do not. The ball skills can come later.

I didn't just play junior league football as a kid. Although my school was a selective one that took boarders and was run along the lines of a traditional public school, it was undeniably slap bang in the middle of a football-mad city. Rugby stood no chance.

Yet I didn't enjoy school football so much, even though it was the domain where there was most success to be had. I played among team-mates who were inherently faster, stronger and more athletic than the opposition. It was that sort of school and my peer group during its halcyon days were national soccer, basketball and swimming champions. The background to becoming national soccer champions doesn't actually make for much of a story save that, largely due to the reflected glory from an all-conquering school side, at the age of seventeen I found myself representing an England Schools XI at the junior World Cup in Belgium.

It wasn't perhaps the most representative of English Schools sides. The England Schools authorities didn't normally bother selecting an Under-17 squad other than for the purposes of this tournament, which was played only every four years. As a result, the selectors drew very heavily from teams who had dominated the previous year's national schools championship. Add to this the fact that by seventeen most of the promising young footballers had either left school, due to a lack of academic interest or achievement, or had been lured out of education by the professional clubs (lest they demonstrate the ability during adult life to formulate sentences, I heard it once suggested) and it wouldn't take Franz Beckenbauer to deduce that this wasn't the strongest team to be sent overseas by the English Schools FA. Still, playing for your country is playing for your country. It just required a study of the opposition rather than your team-mates to convince yourself of that.

The England squad was chaperoned throughout its stay in Belgium by a gaggle of ESFA representatives who, although drawn from different parts of the country, seemed to me uniform in their semi-geriatric deportment and refusal to remove blazers when temperatures were reaching into the nineties (it was Belgium's hottest summer for seventy-four years). The only other way to describe these guardians of the nation's footballing future was as a clueless, bigoted and humourless example of all that was ever wrong with English football.

By the time the England squad had larked its way off the team bus and into its section of the campus just outside Brussels, where all the teams were based, it should have been apparent that other countries were taking a more professional approach to the tournament. The Italian team had been spotted on one of the nearby training pitches doing a set of elaborate stretching exercises that had drawn hoots of derision from our bus. Fancy getting dressed up in the same kit to go to a yoga class together.

Still, this was not nearly as suspect as the German players giving each other massages around the swimming pool. The abuse hurled from our bus was xenophobic and homophobic in a manner that only young British males abroad can truly attain. With hindsight, our only plea in mitigation would be the deep-rooted communal anxiety triggered by the dangerously skimpy swimming trunks on view.

Whatever unspoken unease there was within our ranks became a cold-sweating silence at the section of the campus where the Israeli team were staying. Armed guards! The catcalls suddenly stopped and by the time we disembarked the school trip jocularity had all but evaporated.

To emphasise its utter lack of professionalism and organisation, the England squad had arrived in Belgium only the night before our first game. Our opponents, strongly fancied Nigeria, had been in the country acclimatising for two weeks. The daily temperatures were more African than English anyway, but in our juvenile smugness (and that goes for the Blazers too) no one mentioned the fact, let alone voiced any concern.

This is probably a good time to point out that, notwithstanding the popular assumption that only now are the African nations emerging as an international footballing force, at junior level they have been contenders for years. Nigeria had actually won the preceding tournament and this time around had a squad containing a number of players who had already been picked up by some top French, Dutch and German (funny, no English) professional clubs.

England started the game well. After a frantic opening twenty minutes during which we threw ourselves at everything that moved, we took the lead with a free header from our centre back. It was particularly encouraging that the goal stemmed from a corner routine we had worked on. In fact, it was our only pre-arranged set piece, but we still felt like part of a squad of

European soccer sophisticates as we nonchalantly jogged back to the centre circle and the Nigerians argued among themselves.

We spent the next twenty-five minutes chasing shadows as the opposition suddenly stepped up several gears and began to run around us, behind us and increasingly through us at will. We managed to hold them to a single goal during this period, making the scoreline at the break a respectable 1–1.

I remember the half-time team talk, with a backing track courtesy of the lousy brass band on the pitch outside: 'Get tighter . . .'

'Get stuck in more . . .'

'Talk to each other . . .' (Funny time to start analysing interpersonal relationships I thought).

'Fanny around with it [the ball, I think] less in midfield . . .,' urged the Blazers.

I felt honoured to be privy to such sophisticated strategising. We were halfway through a match against the world champions with honours even and everything to play for. Yet the obvious reality to myself and I'm sure every other non-Blazer in the room was that we had already been shown up as utterly inferior. To make things worse, with forty-five minutes still to run during the middle of the day, we were physically knackered and our opponents were not.

The final scoreline was 4–1, which in no way flattered Nigeria. The closest thing I heard to an excuse for our drubbing came from one of the Blazers who mumbled after the match that there were no such thing as birth certificates in Nigeria and 'most of those big black b— were about ten years older than our lads.'

Stung by the inadequacy of our performance in the opening game, the England team at least played with determination in its match against France forty-eight hours later. The gulf in footballing pedigree was every inch as marked, but due to some poor finishing by the otherwise delightfully skilful French forwards and some brave play by our keeper there was still no score as the game went into its final ten minutes. Then the alleged heat factor kicked in again, or so the Blazers claimed. It ended up 3–0 to France.

We were stunned. How could this happen? The gulf in individual technique and tactical subtlety had been apparent in both games, but the unanimous verdict of the Blazers in each case was that only our opponents' lesser discomfort at the high temperatures had decided the outcome. If the argument that much of France has a similar climate to England served to weaken this analysis, then our subsequent 1–0 defeat by Finland demolished it. We finished bottom of our preliminary group.

By the mid to late 1980s, of course, the debate over why the full England team had for years been tumbling down the world rankings was one we were all familiar with. Falling attendances, trouble on the terraces and the woeful performances of the national team dominated the opinion columns of the sports pages. Among the wailing and gnashing of teeth, it was conventional wisdom that a core problem was the way our schoolboy footballers were coached. I had never doubted the validity of the argument, but as a seventeen-year-old it hadn't occurred to me that I might be a running and tackling example of the malaise.

The eight teams who had been eliminated from the competition in the preliminary round and the eight qualifying teams went on to play separate knockout competitions. We were outclassed by the Dutch (2–0) in the next match. However, after a couple of bruising victories against tired-looking Republic of Ireland and Belgian sides, we ultimately found ourselves placed an almost respectable eleventh out of the original sixteen teams in the tournament.

The game against Belgium had been won on penalties amid some excitement given the large home crowd. Sadly I don't remember feeling any great thrill. I do recall feeling faintly embarrassed at the quality of the football throughout the scoreless ninety minutes and extra time. As the Belgians had scheduled their last match on an afternoon when there were no other games, the other teams in the tournament had been forced to watch us plunder away for a whole two hours.

I felt as if we were the most dour and predictable footballing stereotype imaginable. Yet we missed our chance to shine principally because of the ignorant and outdated system we were playing under. That and an arrogant lack of circumspection among those charged with guiding us.

At least losing 9–0 to Dynamo Stoneycroft left some room for having fun.

I don't think that any of my team-mates from that tournament made it into professional football. For me, the upshot was that at seventeen I'd had enough of FA coaches and playing the ball *into the channels*. I'd completely lost interest in playing at anything approaching a high level and decided that university was a more interesting option than trying to make it as a footballer.

Oxford University has a student population of about 12,000. Even if soccer is far from the most popular sport, therefore, the Blues soccer team is usually able to turn out some fairly useful players, aided by student timetables which allow for a rigorous training programme, outstanding facilities and the other benefits which a university with one of the most famous sporting traditions in the world can offer.

Having gone up to Oxford determined to concentrate on non-sporting pastimes, I was a reluctant debutant (although obviously not as reluctant as I thought I was) in the Blues side during the second week of my first term. To my delight, I found myself in a side where I was no longer shackled by the ignorance or the pressures that had already so alienated me from the game. In a cosmopolitan side (two Scots, two Welshmen, one Greek, one Canadian, one American and one Gambian) that wasn't exactly short on intelligence, the emphasis was always on passing the ball, while the team talks and after-match discussions were a cliché-free zone. All very clever, you might think, but in fact just good fun for a change.

I must confess that it was less due to prowess on the pitch and more due to an alleged historical pre-eminence (well, Oxford did win the FA Cup in about 1878) that we enjoyed a fixture list against a collection of top amateur sides, forces sides and the reserve teams of a handful of professional clubs. It was during these latter fixtures that my new footballing world and my childhood footballing memories would collide.

For their annual match against Oxford, clubs such as Spurs and Arsenal would send out reserve sides consisting mostly of younger players and relatively few star names. The Arsenal side that lined up with Charlie Nicholas and Niall Quinn in attack and Michael Thomas in midfield was a notable exception. Fortunately, the Gunners showed some charity by including Gus Caesar and Perry Groves in the same team.

Most of these younger players had come through the working-class football factory I have described already. Football was likely to be their one hope of a life free of the struggles of their parents. It goes without saying that my Oxford team-mates (notwithstanding any egalitarian noises from the university admissions department) were certainly not from that world and to a man were guaranteed secure futures if they so desired. The contrast in players' backgrounds could not have been greater yet, with the young professionals full of pace and skill but the older Oxford players strong and tactically sound, these were always good-natured and closely fought games.

One year a particularly fresh-faced Arsenal side played with a young black centre forward who, although full of running, may as well have been on a different planet to his team-mates. Attack after Arsenal attack broke down as he either wandered offside, misplaced his lay-offs or simply failed to be where he was meant to be. The frustrations around him and on the touchline were evident and, as the game wore on and the insults from his team-mates got louder, the forward's head began to drop. I don't remember him even calling for the ball in the second half. With an image in my head of the poor kid being sent back on the train to a council estate somewhere, his dream of breaking away from a poor background shattered, I found myself feeling deeply sorry for the guy I was marking.

A couple of times, as we stood in isolation on the halfway line waiting for his next opportunity to run offside, I tried to start some light-hearted small talk. But he never said a word – just blankly stared back at me. What was he thinking? Why wouldn't he speak? Was he shy? Perhaps he despised my apparent privileges? Maybe he was just no good at small talk? I desperately wanted to tell him that I wasn't as divorced from his reality as he might think. That I knew how painful it was to grow up desperately wanting to be a footballer and being cursed by the knowledge, whatever self-doubt or the weight of statistics might tell you, that it wasn't quite an impossible ambition.

With ten minutes remaining and the score at 1–0 to Arsenal, we were pressing for an equaliser. Then a long clearance torpedoed the ball back into our half some fifteen yards behind where we were standing. I had anticipated the clearance and had dropped off a good five yards while the ball was in the air. As it landed I was already adjusting my stride to play the ball back to the goalkeeper. Then, out of nowhere, the young centre forward appeared like a blur. He pushed the ball into his path with his right foot and with his next touch, as he arrived at the edge of the penalty area, slammed it into the far bottom corner of the net.

Slightly stunned by the brilliance of what had gone before, Oxford kicked off. The ball was relayed backwards through the team and as my fellow centre back took a short pass from the left he looked up for a colleague to hit further upfield. In a flash the same Arsenal centre forward whipped the ball off his toe and with an almost instantaneous second touch pushed the ball back across me as I ran across to cover. By the time I'd halted my run and turned back inside, the ball was nestling in the same bottom left-hand corner. Two stunning goals in a minute. Yet the praise from his team-mates had both times been muted. One sensed that the damage to relations was irreparable.

At the final whistle, I tried one last time to spark a friendly exchange. Surely he must be feeling a bit more cheerful now.

'A few more of those and you'll be in the first team,' I grinned.

The same stare. He hadn't even smiled when the goals went in. This kid was resigned to his fate. 'I wouldn't talk to me either,' I thought.

The Arsenal team coach left as soon as they had changed and so, as tended to be the case if there were no guests to entertain, the atmosphere in the bar after the match was distinctly raucous. Several jugs of beer had been consumed before thoughts turned back to the game. Our American goalkeeper, Rick, slurred:

'That was some f— goal their third one.'

'What about the second?' I asked. 'The kid did nothing else all game though. I actually felt quite sorry for him.'

'Jesus, those other Arsenal guys *hated* him. And did you check out his name? That's all he f— needed,' said Rick.

'I thought it was Crowley or Goaley or something.'

'They were calling him Coley . . . His name was Andy Cole. I read the team sheet . . . He's a black guy and his name's Andy COAL!!' convulsed Rick. The table roared with laughter.

'Poor guy,' I thought. 'Sixteen years old and it's all downhill from here.' I silently congratulated myself on having avoided the same disappointment.

no, no, not nantes

LYNNE TRUSS

A Day in the Life - Glenn Hoddle
Sunday Times, June 2000

I usually get up and get started at about 7 a.m. I don't sleep too well despite the tablets, so it's good to take the early shift in the showers, before Big Ron's aftershave has made its daily appearance! But I'm doing well. They're pleased with me. Personally, I can hear the word 'France' these days without bursting into tears. Whereas whisper 'Al Fayed' anywhere near Kevin, and that poor confused man hits trees with his bare fists.

Some of the rehabilitation work they do here is very exciting – pioneering, in fact. For example, we are taken on special night-time visits to supermarkets and car show-rooms, and we pretend to open them, and then, when they hand over the cheque, we receive a massive electric shock so that we don't want to do it ever again. That's quite clever, isn't it? Sometimes they catch us off-guard and shove football programmes at us, which is a bit unfair. I signed one myself, handing the pen back automatically to the wrong person, and I got a three-dinner ban, no argument.

But you can divine their purpose, overall. 'Strip away those harmful layers of behaviour,' they tell us in our group sessions. The best bit is when they make us stand on an imaginary line, in pairs, chewing and looking agitated, in outdoor coats. 'Go on, chew gum! Fold your arms! Come on Glenn, look agitated, I know you can do it! Now point and shout!' And then they turn a big mirror on us, and the idea is that we suddenly see (through a glass, darkly) how mad we look, and stop in horror. It's a brutal method but it works brilliantly, except on poor old Martin O'Neill. Lovely bloke, Martin, but no amount of aversion therapy stops him leaping up and down in a deranged salmon-upstream sort of manner. Talk about a lost cause.

Once a week we give imaginary press conferences – press conferences with a difference, because we say exactly what we mean, and we're banned from saying 'Take nothing away from the other team', which makes the whole thing a lot more difficult! For example, I'm giving one tonight, reflecting on the lucky breaks we got in the 1998 World Cup in France – which is the one I always give. 'Come on Glenn,' they say. 'Courage. Let's have it again.' But every time I give it, it changes a bit, and some of the black fog clears from that enormous event.

I mean to say, rejoice in the Lord always and again I say rejoice – no one ever saw anything remotely like that World Cup for upsets and disgruntled Brazilians. Not since Onan in the Bible had so many seeds hit the deck and withered. Who met us in the last sixteen at Bordeaux? Japan. At Lyon in the quarter-finals? South Korea. We went through the lot like a bayonet through a sherry trifle. We were serene, controlled, magnanimous, blessed. And by the end of it, we were literally almost bored with winning. David Seaman started reading *Jane Eyre* during matches, and as far as I know, he finished it. Reader, it was unbelievable. We had to keep changing our return flights. 'You'll never believe this, but we've got Japan next,' we told the airline. 'So what shall we say?' they replied. 'Another week?' And we'd say 'Well, yes.'

I think it's understandable to have a crisis of belief in a situation like that. I mean, a real God wouldn't go so far to prove his existence, would he? Not in such a showy, obvious way. Ergo, he didn't exist. Getting Paraguay in the semi-finals was the final straw for me, faith-wise. No God-fearing person has ever been put to a test like that.

But it's funny, I always get to the same Paraguay bit in the imaginary press conference, and then I stop. I have this vision of little Robbie Fowler racing towards the goal with the ball, after a genius pass from Beckham. Fowler beats one! He beats two! It's just him and the goalie. For a guaranteed place in the final! Chilavert lunges! And then – what? It all goes black, and as I rejoin the world, the guys here are clapping supportively with tears in their eyes, and I'm saying 'What happened next? For pity's sake, what happened next?'

They're always telling us here, there's life after football. Look at Gazza's career on *Animal Hospital*, they say. Evidently 'And what's up with *you*, bonny lad?' has become a national catch-phrase. And there's only one thing more bizarre than Stuart Pearce becoming a star of *Ready Steady Cook*; it's that we've all accepted it without a quibble. As wee Gordon Strachan pointed out in the TV room the other afternoon, 'Aye, you cannae picture yon psycho *without* the pinny noo.'

But as for me – well, I just can't let it go. Fowler beats one. He beats two. Out comes Chilavert. Oh, *Eli, Eli, lema sabachthani* (Matthew, xxvii, 46). My God, My God, why hast thou forsaken me?

July 8, 1998. St Denis, Paris. Stade de France. Half past something. And then nothing. If God be for us, who can be against us? Whatever it was Robbie Fowler did, it's amazing how much care and support you need, to confront a thing like *that*.

Extract from Questionnaire – Robbie Fowler
Sunday Magazine, 1998
Q: Which words do you over-use?
A: How do you mean?

Q: Words you use a lot.

A: Oh. 'Over here, I'm inside the box'?

Q: Right.

A: 'On me 'ead'?

Q: We'll leave that for now. Can you describe yourself in three words?

A: Robert. Bernard. Fowler.

Q: Swear in a foreign language?

A: Why? Who came in?

Profile of Alan Shearer

Five One Three One Magazine, October 1998

A dog barks outside Alan Shearer's house in a wealthy suburb of Newcastle. It is a mournful sound. 'Woof!' it says. 'Woof, woof'. A hearse passes quietly, black and long. A plane flies high overhead, scoring the sky like – like a thin white slightly furry line on a bright blue background. Sports writers are not entirely without literary sensibility, you know. We notice things, and endow them with significance. Outside Alan Shearer's house I pause and make notes. I employ the dramatic present tense, relentlessly. Dog. Hearse. Plane. Is Alan Shearer a dog barking mournfully at the deserted late-summer afternoon? Is he dead? Or is he just away on holiday? These are some of the things I am here to find out.

I find Alan in his trophy room with his leg in plaster to the hip, a neck brace, and an enormous split shoe on one foot.

'Just my luck,' he shrugs, miserably. 'Only slipped in the bath, man. Out of action for another six month.' He holds up his hand, to reveal fingers strapped together. 'Did that beggar feedin' the babby, like.'

Shearer looks so young in the flesh. Yet so vulnerable. Dog? Hearse? Plane? I plump for hearse. But the dog barks again, insistently. *Woof, woof.* Damn. I liked the dog. *Woof.* The phone rings and I make another note. 'Ditch colour writing,' I write. 'Too formulaic.' And with this devastating insight, I find that I have surprised . . . even myself.

'Have you come to talk about the latest *tranche* of injuries?' Alan's wife whispers when he leaves the room on crutches to check the state of some creosote in the garden. She has interrupted my reverie, and I look at her blankly. I mean, if I gave up this dog-hearse-plane-phone malarkey, what might follow? This is a high-level career at stake, you know, lady. Several hundred pounds a year from broadsheets alone. 'Don't depress him, will you?' she continued. 'It's just that after twisting his knee at the World Cup opening ceremony – well, you know.'

So I sigh, and get down to it. But it's so boring talking to footballers. How do they always feel if they're losing? 'Disappointed, obviously.' God almighty. How do they feel if they're winning? 'Cautiously optimistic.' Whereas not many people know this, but I wrote a novel once. And it was bloody good. It was about the well-muscled men who soldered rivets on the *Titanic*, and it made brilliant play with the metaphors of bonding, sparks and goggles.

I join Alan at the fence he's painting, stricken with sadness for a career that's gone so horribly wrong. Mine.

'So how the hell did you manage to injure yourself at the opening ceremony, Alan?' I ask pleasantly, man-to-man. 'Months on the treatment tables, months of training, you hop sideways to avoid a stray bit of baguette wrapper and *crunch*!, you're writhing in agony again, missing the whole bloody tournament. Shall I just put "disappointed obviously" or are you actually going to say something interesting?'

He looks at me as if I'm mad.

'No, seriously,' I say. 'The readers of *Five One Three One* are such sad sacks they actually want to know how it felt for you watching from the sidelines in France as Sheringham and

Fowler and Andy Cole scored all those goals in the World Cup against second-rate teams who had peaked defeating Brazil and Germany and were now too shagged to run about. I mean, Paraguay as nemesis? Don't make me laugh.'

He holds the brush in his one good hand, and is about to speak when I notice something. 'You missed a bit, Alan,' I say, indicating a patch of fence. The dog barks, and I make a note. 'Is that your dog, by the way?'

'Get out,' he says. 'Piss off.'

'Alan,' I protest. (I like calling him Alan.)

'Get out,' echoes his lovely wife.

'Why, Alan?' I say. But he pokes me with his crutch, and I don't know what comes over me, but I grab hold of it and push, and he topples over backwards.

'No!' he shouts, over a loud crunching sound (bad news for the Shearer coccyx, I fear). And then it all happens very fast, and in the time it takes to ask myself 'Would Ernest Hemingway have put up with this sort of thing?' I'm outside the front gate.

'I'll have you know I sometimes write for *The Times Literary Supplement*!' I yell indignantly through the bars. But they've gone back inside.

The dog barks.

The hearse drives slowly past, this time from right to left.

As if the direction of the hearse makes any difference to poor old Alan Shearer, eh? I construct a complex analogy about rearranging the furniture on the *Titanic*, rearranging the dogs in a sinking hearse that's crashed changing direction, wasting a career.

And then I sit on a low wall, waiting to see if a crisp packet or old newspaper will blow past. Because if you wait long enough for incidental colour stuff in this sports feature-writing game, it usually comes along, in the end.

Extract from Questionnaire - Robbie Fowler
Sunday Magazine, 1998

Q: What do you want written on your tombstone?

A: 'Over here, I'm inside the box.'

Q: That's very good.

A: Is it? 'On me 'ead'?

From How We Met - Paul Gascoigne and Graeme Le Saux
Independent on Sunday, May 2000

'We never really took to each other at first, like,' admits Paul Gascoigne, giving his best mate Graeme Le Saux a friendly hug for our photographer. 'I thought he were a bit of a girlie, to be brutally frank.'

It's funny to think there was a time when the reputations of these two football internationals were almost never linked. Paul Gascoigne's best friend was not Graeme Le Saux – it was a drinking crony famous for multiple stomachs. Meanwhile Le Saux's best friend was *Miller's Antiques Guide*. But this was before events at the last World Cup changed everything. The shock of losing in the semi-final to Paraguay after the easiest run in the tournament's history changed many England players in unpredictable ways. The ordination of Tony Adams had its surreal side, for many.

Paul Gascoigne's saintly *Animal Hospital* career is certainly a case in point. But he's a pro, if nothing else. 'What's up with *you*, bonny lad?' our photographer asks him jovially. And instead of hitting him (as he would have done in former times), Gazza laughs, slaps him playfully on the back and tells him how touching it is to spend so much time with poorly pets.

LE SAUX: To be honest, I used to think Paul was a complete nutcase. Our paths would cross occasionally, but his main interaction with me in international training was to knock my

Bumper Book of Guardian Crosswords out of my hand and flush it down the lav, so I can't say he was my favourite bloke, no.

Obviously it was when I pulled him off Robbie Fowler in the Paraguay game that we found ourselves welded together by the white heat of destiny. July 8, 1998. St Denis. Half past something. Paraguay are three goals down already, and Robbie gets tackled in the penalty area. 'Penalty!' yells the crowd. 'Penalty!' we all cheer on the pitch. It's brilliant. Like a dream. The final is in sight.

But then it all goes wrong. Instead of rolling about on the ground, Robbie jumps up and makes 'No, no, hang on' gestures at the ref. Now, he claims he can't remember why he did that, and I can't say I blame him. But it was insane, insane. 'What the fuck is this?' we all ask ourselves (even those of us who don't usually swear). 'It's a fucking penalty! Ignore him, ref! Give us the fucking penalty!' The adrenalin's pumping a bit, of course, and our blood is up, and the crowd is roaring, and the ref hasn't made up his mind yet, but the next thing we know, Paul's thumped him. Gone up to little Robbie Fowler and thumped him. The crowd goes mad. They thought it was all over. And it certainly is now.

Steve McManaman pushes Paul in the chest for hitting his sidekick, which is when I wade in to stop everybody, and Tony Adams rushes up covered in blood and says 'What the fuck's it got to do with you, four eyes?' – and I just punch him on the nose and the upshot is we're all sent off, and Hoddle has the breakdown, and it's all deeply, deeply regrettable. Fucking ref sent five of us off. Five. Paraguay walked it.

GASCOIGNE: What's he been sayin' about me? Don't I get to talk about him? Girlie swot with his long words.

LE SAUX: No, I'll handle it. Look, there's a doggy with a limp over there, Paul. Over there.

GASCOIGNE: Where?

LE SAUX: There.

The only good thing that came out of this was the change in Paul. I'm doing all right now, although I lost interest in the antiques, couldn't see the point in all that old junk any more. Things look very different when Paraguay have beaten you 15–3. But I don't blame myself for what happened. Luckily for the rest of us, Paul took the blame entirely on himself, and we all really respect him for that, as well as secretly hating him for thinking of it. Because suddenly – peculiarly – he's a big hero, and the rest of us are just has-beens.

Relative Values – David Seaman and his Mum
Sunday Times, November 1998

MRS SEAMAN: Oh, it was lovely, the World Cup. Seeing our David singing the national anthem, in all those lovely oranges and greens. You still using the Wash 'n' Go, dear?

DAVID SEAMAN: Mum!

MRS S: Your hair looked lovely anyway. You said we'd only see you the three times, David. But it turned out to be six, didn't it? And how many goals did you let in, David, overall?

DAVID S: Fifteen.

MRS S: Yes, but they were all in the one game, so they don't count. I hate seeing David jump about. When it's your own flesh and blood, that's natural. And I love to see him pick up a Penguin Classic, because he never was an imaginative child. So I was very happy with the World Cup, *Jane Eyre* and all, right up to that last match. Who was it, David? The last match?

DAVID S: Paraguay.

MRS S: I've been making this Spitfire pilot outfit for him, but he won't wear it. Tell him he'd look lovely in it, he won't believe me because I'm his mother. Why doesn't he make more of his looks? That moustache is so dashing, David. Say 'Chocks away', I tell him, but he just won't. I did him a complete *Seaman of Arabia*, curly-handled dagger, yards of sheeting. But what happened to that? Dusters. What was the other outfit I did for you, David?

DAVID S: I don't remember.

MRS S: Yes you do.

DAVID S: Mum!

MRS S: It was *Indiana Seaman*, with a whip and everything.

DAVID S: Oh, mum.

Final extract from Questionnaire – Robbie Fowler

Sunday Magazine, 1998

Q: Who on TV would you most like to be?

A: Alan Hansen.

Q: Really? Alan 'Brainy' Hansen? You don't see any obstacles?

A: You mean I'm not Scottish.

Q: If you wanted to apologise to someone, the whole country for example, whose dreams you helped shatter, how would you do it?

A: Sorry?

Q: Look, here's an easy one. Where do you wear your hat?

A: How do you mean?

Q: On your head, Robbie. On your head!

A: What's wrong?

Q: I can't do this any more. Would you rather do 'What's on my Mantelpiece?' instead? I'm quite easy, either way.

A: All right. I'm up for that. What's on your mantelpiece?

My Favourite Client: Publicist Jamie Beckett on Paul Gascoigne

Observer Life, January 1999

I called Paul immediately after the Paraguay match, when he was still in hiding in Spain. And I said to him, 'How would you like to be more popular than if you'd scored the winning goal at the World Cup?' He put the phone down, and I rang him back. He put the phone down, and I rang him back again. 'I just want to say three things to you, Paul,' I said. 'Repentance. Forgiveness. And Cleaning Up.'

I won three awards for Paul, and rightly so. In a country stupefied by misery, I was the sole person able to accentuate the positive, and to spot the rather obvious fact that football supporting is mainly, in any case, about the sweet, sweet agony of communal grief. Grief was extremely popular – ergo, Paul could go from public enemy to popular martyr in two weeks flat. Which thanks to me, he did. I used to say to him 'Sackcloth and Ashes R Us, mate. Think how fantastic it will make everybody feel, to redeem somebody as stupid and violent as you!' Being a bit thick, he didn't believe it at first. But when I got him National Schizophrenia Week, and an invitation to Number 10, he had to admit it was working. Professionally speaking, that period with Paul was simply the best time I've ever, ever had.

'I want me old life back,' he would whinge in the early days. But as I pointed out, he could hardly go back to Rangers, what with Scotland beating Paraguay in the final and winning the Cup. For a man who didn't know much about irony, that would still be more horror than he could stand. And I refused to let him return to his old light-the-blue-fart-and-retire lifestyle. So I got him Graeme Le Saux as a mate, a good dentist, and a new haircut. Five Bellies wasn't allowed to see him until he was down to Two and a Half Bellies. Which kept him out of the picture for quite a while.

You see, the way I saw it, Gareth Southgate misses a penalty at Euro 96, and he gets to make a pizza commercial with Waddle and Pearce. I just saw the way the wind was blowing. Gazza destroys England's dead certainty to win the World Cup – and of course, he has the choice to become a laughing stock, too. But how about he becomes the focus of a national emotional outpouring on a scale of the death of Princess Diana? We put him on chat-shows with Le Saux, and told him to make with the famous tear-ducts. But take nothing away from Paul, it was his own idea to cling to Graeme's sleeve, sobbing 'Thirty years of hurt, like. Never stopped me dreamin'.' I'll never forget the chills I got when he did that. 'The boy's a star!' I said. 'And this could only happen with football.'

Paul wept. Graeme snivelled. And the whole country clung to each other, with tears streaming. It was brilliant. They wept for themselves, for Paul's agony, for all their football aspirations, for life itself. Thirty years of hurt. Thirty years. Brilliant. Looking back on it, I'm just so glad we didn't *win* the World Cup. God knows how anybody deals with a thing like that.

watching *the unbearable lightness of being instead of chelsea–arsenal*

HUGO BORST

I

Sunday 21 September 1997

She follows the legs, not the ball. That's something, given that she doesn't like football. You can find that unfathomable, you can hold it against someone, you can despise someone for it, but when it's your wife it's very different.

It's a missed chance, I put it to her, because love is at its most beautiful when a man and a woman are watching a football match on television together.

'You used to watch with me sometimes,' I say.

'I used to be in love with you,' she says.

'Not any more?'

'You know. I love you. That's worth much more.'

'Your love isn't unconditional any more.'

'Just put the video on. We've had this discussion a hundred times. You don't watch *EastEnders* with me either. You don't have to. In fact I don't want you to. You'd ask stupid questions, you'd distract me.'

After twenty minutes of play I have to leave Chelsea–Arsenal. It's like suddenly having to stop making love because the dishwasher has to be emptied; knowing that you will not come.

'Oh, oh, not coming just for once, what a disaster,' she says.

As I put the tape of *The Unbearable Lightness of Being* in the video, I think that it's a damned shame, because Dennis is always extra motivated when he plays against Gullit. He will never say it out loud, but just as almost all the great Dutch players are not keen on Gullit, Dennis doesn't like him much either.

In Italy, at Inter, when Bergkamp was a topic of debate, when all those fantastic moves and goals for Ajax and Holland seemed to have been collectively forgotten, and in Italy sports journalists, coaches, team-mates and directors were dragging his name through the mud, just then Gullit decided to say in an Italian newspaper that as an immigrant you had to adjust to the country where you worked, and that if you didn't, you would never integrate. When I confronted Dennis – by then liberated by Arsenal – with Gullit's criticism in August 1995, a silence fell. Briefly he glanced aside at Henrita, with her eyes she smiled at him, and then he began to talk.

'What was the purpose of a remark like that? Why does he say something like that in the press? Does he want to help me out of the pit, or do I have to sink even deeper? If it's meant as advice, then call me. It seems that the remark wasn't meant for me, but for himself. With Bryan Roy he once did something like that too. I'm not asking for support or solidarity, you know, but this doesn't make me any better. And he doesn't know me at all. Only the other members of my generation at Ajax know me a little. All those people who want to give their opinion about me should do it in person. Otherwise they should keep their mouths shut. Because they don't understand. And only one person did call me with personal advice. Twice, in fact. Faas Wilkes [the seventy-four-year-old all-time highest scorer of the Dutch team, who played for Inter himself nearly fifty years ago]. Very sweet, I thought. He wanted to give me heart. Something like: "Boy, you go your own way. You are a good footballer. It will come right." I thought that was marvellous. The point is, when I was in Italy I really didn't walk around on clogs.'

It's a meaningful, intelligent answer. You hear indignation, but Dennis isn't vengeful. He is not excessively proud, he is not a boy full of hate, but he will fight for himself. Whether he is attacked verbally by malicious ex-colleagues, or hunted by cruel defenders – he can cope. And if referees won't protect him then he'll protect himself.

'I learned from Van Basten how to give out,' he told me during the European Championships of 1992 in Sweden. 'A striker has to. When I'm in form I'll "play" with a defender. Small things. Hook his foot if the ball's not around. Dirty little things like that, which make the guy lose concentration. If it works he gets aggressive and then in the next one-on-one he'll dive in quicker. Or he'll commit an unnecessary foul, which of course I'll have seen coming.'

He grinned.

With the remote control I make the footballers disappear. Sometimes you have to make sacrifices. Maybe later I will be granted sex in return.

Has Dennis seen *The Unbearable Lightness of Being*? I don't think he has read Kundera's novel. I hope Tony Adams recommends it to him.

'I think,' Dennis Bergkamp told me eleven years ago in a whisper, 'that *The Good, the Bad and the Ugly* is a good film.'

March 1987 was my first of five lengthy interviews with Dennis. Johan Cruijff, the Ajax manager, had surprised everyone by selecting the unremarkable youth player for his European debut. Dennis, seventeen years old, was really supposed to be at school, but he was doing so well in class that the headmaster willingly let him travel with Ajax to Sweden. Two months later Dennis, alongside Van Basten, Rijkaard and Wouters, won the European Cup-Winners' Cup in Athens.

On his entrée into the Dutch league, in December 1986,

Dennis – like Cruijff, Van Basten and Rijkaard on their debuts – had scored a goal. Because of the typical Ajax tradition that good players score in their first match for the club, he aroused expectations. During our first conversation Dennis told me quietly what Frank Rijkaard – whom he had not dared look in the eye for a long time – had told him in the bath after his first match. 'You've got a golden future ahead of you, boy.'

Dennis went red as he told me this. He is the first and only Amsterdammer in my life who isn't bursting with self-confidence. If there's one Amsterdammer who has a right to be cocky, it's him; but he never wanted to.

Pale and silent he sat opposite me. I remember Dennis's clothes; sober, dated – very uncommon for Ajax players, who have kidded themselves that they are part of the centre of the universe. I think that Dennis's mother still bought his clothes at C&A, maybe he still had to wear out his older brothers' trousers. His parents were not rich. His father (an electrician) was sometimes called out of bed at night, and when he came back he had earned twenty-five guilders (£7), Dennis noted. Dennis confessed that he was ashamed in the beginning to be paid 1,000 guilders for a victory (in an hour and a half). The first thing Dennis did when he could afford it was have a house built for his parents outside Amsterdam. It took at least four years for Dennis to wear a jacket by Versace or someone like that, but he has never become flamboyant, let alone dandyesque.

In the time that he played for Ajax he built a wall around himself that was as invisible as it was impregnable. Around him there was always silence, silence that his team-mates respected, silence that only Dennis himself broke, often with a dry-as-dust remark that made everybody really laugh. His sense of humour is subtle, ironic, sharp-witted, understated and therefore of a higher order. In the Dutch team he is renowned for his witty moments.

Sometimes he will lend himself to football humour – or a civilised form of it. Not long ago a few Arsenal players were signing a cap. The space was rather limited. Before Ray Parlour wrote his own autograph and passed the pen to Dennis, he asked: 'Do you have a big one, Dennis?' It is an unambiguous remark, but Dennis frowned briefly, said nothing, let his eyes wander demonstratively towards his crotch, pouted his lips and looked at Parlour with a glance that said, How can you ask that? Wright, Overmars and the other players laughed heartily at Dennis's body language.

Sometimes Dennis lands briefly on earth. Although the image is not entirely a happy one with him, he has occupied a height well above the other players. And that's not arrogance, quite the opposite. Dennis will be modest all his life. Given the choice, he seeks seclusion. As long as I have been following him, a desire for anonymity has been inherent in everything he does. He does his best to appear cheery, a good colleague, boyish and sociable, but it often takes him a lot of trouble. In well over two seasons at Arsenal, he and Platt have gone to some restaurant or other once. That the restaurant was called Quaglino's, that the restaurant is hip, passes him by, what does it matter, he would rather be with Henrita. Dennis is from another world, don't ask me which one, but he is not an inhabitant of the football world. Being different is allowed in football only if you are better or special on the pitch. Fortunately he is. His play for Holland and Arsenal corresponds with the height that he permits himself off the field. Nick Hornby recently summed it up best in *Hard Gras*, the Dutch magazine. He suspects Dennis of having three feet.

However beautiful and exciting Juliette Binoche may be, my thoughts constantly wander off towards Bergkamp and Arsenal. My wife knows this. When she goes to the toilet, she turns up the volume, and as a precautionary measure takes the remote control with her. A little later she shouts: 'What do you think the score is at Arsenal?'

I burst out laughing. Our laugh-life is showing no signs of wear yet.

It's just that Dennis was born on 10 May 1969 in the Vierheemskinderenstraat in Amsterdam. Both Dennis and the hero of his youth, Glenn Hoddle, would have benefited from a partnership. I am convinced that the England team and Dennis would make each other world champions. I can't imagine that Holland – with Dennis, without Dennis – will ever be crowned at a World Cup. In 1974 and 1990 we thought we were unbeatable. We had the best players, maybe we were the best, but we lost to the Germans. Now, too, we think we can become world champions. If we Dutchmen excel at anything it is at immodesty and stubbornness. After the first round Germany awaits. And if we don't go out against our inherited enemy then we will against France, Brazil or Croatia. The only good news for Dennis is that at the World Cup he will surpass Wilkes (35 goals) as Holland's highest scorer.

After Euro 96 Hugh McIlvanney remarked about our national side: 'A lousy Dutch team.' He wouldn't have bet on Holland with someone else's money. 'The Dutch were extremely weak representatives of their own tradition and they didn't have the will to fight their way out of a paper bag,' said McIlvanney.

Compared with the Dutch teams of '74, '78 and not forgetting '88, this generation does lack winners. Jan Wouters was once called Holland's bouncer. I miss him, and men like Van Hanegem, Krol, Neeskens, Wim Jansen, Van Basten, Rijkaard and Ronald Koeman. Best of course is when both components – destruction and creativity – are united in one player, but to win the World Cup, strangely enough, you need more anti-footballers than footballers. We used to have refined destroyers like Suurbier, Rijsbergen and Van Tiggelen. Who fills their role

now? Every man in the Dutch team can play football very well.
But who will compensate for Dennis?

Jesus, what a film. Never say again that the book was better
than the film. *The Unbearable Lightness of Being* might even be
better than Chelsea–Arsenal, I reflect. When she asks me that
later I won't confirm it, of course. I will say that I can't possibly
judge because I didn't see the match.

The main characters Tomas and Tereza are lying in bed.
Tomas has cheated on Tereza again. Tereza can smell that he has
been with someone else. Rage, sadness, you know the kind of
thing. At one point she says angrily and helplessly: 'Oh yes,
Tomas, you've explained a thousand times. There's love and
there's sex. Sex is entertainment, just like football.'

I think about that for a long time.

There's love and there's sex. Sex is entertainment, just like
football.

But is that true? Is football sex? Are they comparable
entities? What does Dennis think? It could be. But football is
love too. Maybe not in the eyes of the footballers who are doing
their jobs, who are disloyal and change clubs every two years,
but the fans – surely they want more than just to be entertained?
A football match isn't an hour and a half of sex, is it? How many
fans don't share their lives with their football club? Their love
doesn't end with the final whistle. There is always desire,
despair, joy and sadness.

'Bastard,' my wife says to Tomas.

'He deceives Tereza, but he does love her,' I say.

'Men,' she says.

When I went to an Arsenal game last season, I found a man
outside the ground who was selling a Number Ten shirt which
bore the name not of Bergkamp but of God. In 1991 Dennis and

I spoke in an Amsterdam café near the Ajax stadium De Meer, since torn down, about his faith. Brought up a Catholic, prayers before meals, to church every Sunday in his childhood, although only at Christmas and Easter in the last couple of years.

'I am convinced that I am being guided from above,' said Dennis.

I expressed my surprise.

'Hard to explain,' he continued. 'It's a feeling. I have a feeling that everything has been determined. But I'm also convinced that I'll get a sign if I say goddamn six times in a row. Of course I swear. I'm fairly human. When I miss chances, for instance. Against Volendam I messed up tap-ins. And at moments like that I think I'm being punished, and the other way around: when I'm lucky, it's a kind of reward or something. Crossing myself at the start of a match or after a goal – I don't do that. If I score, I thank God inside myself.'

For a long time I personally couldn't get enough of players who thanked God after a goal, or who would appeal to Him in an interview. I find Brazilian footballers the most touching. It's the way they talk about Him. The certainty with which they count on Him. And God never lets them down. As if they know something about Him, as if they can manipulate God a little, as if they think: God also knows that two billion people around the world watch the World Cup, so if we cross ourselves after a goal that won't go unnoticed, His name recognition will increase, He knows that. Does that prompt Him to relent and make the Brazilians world champions so often? I often wonder why He doesn't give Carlton Palmer a helping hand. Probably Man isn't God's creation after all, but God is the creation of Man. Don't hold me to that, though.

In recent years there are more and more footballers who are zealous about God. And not the worst ones either. But by now I've had enough of their God-stories. Give me Bergkamp instead. His faith is his own. When a journalist from an evangelical TV station told him that as a famous Dutchman he should bear witness to his religion more, Bergkamp was irritated. 'My faith is my own. I don't have to advertise, do I?' He hates religious exhibitionism just as I do. In last year's Christmas edition of the magazine *Vrij Nederland*, Bergkamp said: 'You see more and more footballers cross themselves when they come onto the field. As long as they do it from conviction I think it's fine. But often I think: "You're just copying the American athletes." And then I instantly think it's worthless.'

When I told Dennis that I'd seen a shirt of his with God on the back, he shrugged his shoulders and remarked that 'luckily in England there's a bit of irony behind it. In Italy they really believe it.'

Why does the sight of Dennis always evoke words like God, divine, heavenly? I find him – fear of flying, moved by the Diana tribute version of 'Candle in the Wind', his contempt for English referees, the odd dive, the greatest difficulty with simple tap-ins – downright earthly. Why all those high-flown comparisons? I mean, what in the name of heaven does Bergkamp have in common with God? Probably Bergkamp's God, like Bergkamp himself, doesn't like beer, coke, nightclubs, porn, adultery and so on, sure, but apart from that there is no similarity. Can God play football at all?

Recently the former Arsenal keeper Bob Wilson came up to Dennis. He told him that he came to the stadium especially for Bergkamp. There are hundreds like that, thousands. What he did match after match in August and September of 1997 was extraordinary. He told me his form was comparable to the way he used to feel on the street: the same guilelessness, everything happening as if by itself. That Dennis thinks that at moments like that he is being guided, I respect, but I can't believe it; I immediately think of a marionette, a man on strings, wooden movements, I think of Steve Bould. Really, Dennis does it strictly with the body which he has been given for a while. Chemistry and intuition are involved, OK, but it all occurs in the body itself. Dennis of all people strikes me as a footballer of flesh and blood. He walks on grass, he performs miracles, but he is tangible, he exists, and one day he will decay. If he is a Saviour then he is one of mortal calibre. Charlie George went, Brady went, and Bergkamp will go too. But the worshippers need not fear. Dennis is a monogamous boy. He told me recently that he won't swap Arsenal for another club. Dennis has come to love the uncomplicated English way that lives in the tackles and the attitude to the game, he admires the sincere love of football. In four years' time at Highbury he will conclude his career, although he does want a couple more playmakers this summer, because he despises opportunism, or as he told me in one of our interviews: 'Behind every kick of the ball there has to be a thought.'

'What are you thinking?' my wife asks.

I throw my arm around her. 'Nothing.'

▐▐

Wednesday 14 January 1998

Less than a minute ago I said that Dennis must score now, because ninety minutes of FA Cup football plus extra time – without goals – is a trial (I say this because I know she likes to hear it), and dammit, Dennis gets the ball outside the penalty area, frees himself, bends his body slightly backwards and sweeps the inside of his instep against the ball, which gains height instantly and sails over goalkeeper Musselwhite into the top corner. 0–1.

'Jesus, Dennis hadn't scored since 4 October,' I tell my wife.

'My birthday,' she says.

'Really?'

'Funny, haha,' she says and lays her head on my chest.

'Who are the whites?' she asks.

'Port Vale.'

With her hand she strokes the skin of my stomach.

'Strange name, Port Vale.'

She rubs up and down over the material of my underpants. What is this? What is going on? She has said that I can watch the last half hour of the match in bed. Not for a moment did I read a sign in this. I hadn't told her that there was a risk of extra time, just because it's impossible to explain why one match does and another doesn't have extra time.

'How small and soft it is,' she grins.

'I can only concentrate on one thing at a time.'

'Rubbish. You men can do it always and anywhere. How long to go?'

'More than a quarter of an hour.'

Sigh.

During the second half of extra time she brings it to life. Port Vale are attacking boisterously. I actually think an erection during a football match is sacrilegious. With me, sex has always stood one rung lower in the hierarchy than football. Sex is entertainment, football is love.

You see: Port Vale promptly score.

'Now it's 1–1. If it stays like this there will be penalties,' I say.

I expect a sigh, but suddenly she throws herself upon me, like a keeper on the ball. 'Come on,' she commands five minutes before the end of the match. She is clasping me tightly. Presses her lips onto mine.

And so we make love during the close of Port Vale–Arsenal, third round of the FA Cup. We lie across the middle of the bed, every now and then I turn my head to the television. It's still 1–1. Penalties.

I see Dixon miss. Jesus, what a bad shot, I think.

'Should have been further in the corner, eh?' she says from beneath me.

'Mind your own business,' I say.

Laughing, fiery, not at all softly she twists my head back in her direction and urges me on.

Is she a little behind now? I never know exactly. It has to be more mechanical, now.

Shit, I think I'm going too fast. Delay. Delay! Usually I think about the introduction of the euro, inflation, falling bond yields, that kind of thing. Missed penalties, it suddenly flashes through my mind. Think about famous missed penalties. Name ten.

Zico, 1986 World Cup against France.

Platini, same match.

Pearce, 1990 World Cup against Germany. I can see the ball flying over the bar.

Waddle, same match.

Southgate, Euro 96 against Germany, saved.

Seedorf, 1998 World Cup qualifier against Turkey, over the bar.

Van Basten, 1992 European Championship against Denmark, to Schmeichel's left – saved.

Don't think about what you're doing. More penalties. But no more pictures come.

Another question. What matters in a penalty? Control. Restraint. That's what it's about. Don't run up too quickly. Choose your corner. Or you can wait to see what the keeper does. Van Basten was good at that. Only Schmeichel didn't fall for it. That cost us the European Championship.

Body bent forward.

I can hear my wife. Thank God. She has made it.

I glance aside one more time. Dennis is ready. It has to go in.

Arsenal has to win the FA Cup. Dennis who dreams of shirts, stadia and Wembley and not of money, Dennis has to win the FA Cup. Dennis has already chosen his corner. I know that for sure. To the left of the keeper, hard, precise, just you watch. With a calm heart I leave Dennis to his fate.

A long run-up, I rear myself up, temples throbbing, a shudder runs through my body, everywhere muscles clench together, I hear myself saying that I love her.

Translated by Simon Kuper.

when scotland do win the world cup

PATRICK BARCLAY

Every visit to Dundee, the sprawling grey waste of an estuary backdrop where I was schooled, involves a pilgrimage to Dens Park. This is where I learned to love football and dark-blue shirts, although the notion of some laboured educational process may be misleading; obsession with Dundee FC came as naturally as interest in girls. It was also instrumental in producing an incorrigible optimist because, when I was fourteen, only a few years into the affair, Dundee won the Scottish League championship for the first time. This was the spring of 1962. The club had been formed in 1893. That works out at sixty-nine years of not being champions. Yet I was surprised only that it had taken them so long and the ensuing autumn, when we sallied forth into the European Cup, was to bring further confirmation of innate superiority.

The scores may stretch your credence. Even we pinched ourselves while absorbing the first. Cologne arrived at Dens and were beaten 8–1 (aggregate 8–5 after a violent and perturbing, but ultimately academic, return match). Sporting Lisbon, having won 1–0 in Portugal, then fell by 4–1. Anderlecht were all but disposed of in the away leg, a match whose course I followed from my bedroom by twiddling the dial of a crackly radio until a Flemish commentator could be identified, loud and unclear yet so gloomy in his pronunciation of words such as 'Gilzean' and 'Penman' that I knew we were doing well. We won 4–1 and could afford to slack a bit at Dens, where the Belgians got away with a 2–1 defeat. The outcome of the semi-final was also decided in the first leg. We were beaten 5–1 by Milan. But there was a perfectly reasonable explanation, for which we were grateful to the *Courier and Advertiser*. Dastardly Italian photographers, stationed behind the goal Dundee were defending, had used flashbulbs, putting our men off at vital moments (the local glamour boys, we presumed, were accustomed to such a filmstar environment and therefore unaffected by any impulse to blink as they kept nodding crosses into our net). It was a lesson in objective and astute journalism that I have never forgotten. Fairness is a Dundonian characteristic. We even accepted, when Dundee were winning the home leg 1–0 but clearly manifesting an inability substantially to alter the aggregate situation, that the aforementioned Alan Gilzean deserved to be sent off for kicking an opponent in the goolies. While wrong, it was Gillie's way of putting the general view that, over two legs, or indeed between them, Milan were the better side.

To my naive mind, however, all the illustrious European clubs who had visited Dens Park had one thing in common. I imagined how impressed they must have been to find that a city of 170,000 inhabitants could feature such a large, characterful and atmospheric stadium.

A few years later I started work and moved to England, got married and had children, and eventually found that to encounter Dens from afar was to see it in a quite different light: as a stark, undeniably provincial ground whose only genuflection to the symmetric ideal was a gently chevron-shaped Archibald Leitch grandstand that had earned the approval of Simon Inglis, football's architectural guru, and constituted the sole whisper of an argument against levelling the entire site and moving Dundee across the road to the more modern and adequate home of their neighbours United. Even today the scale of Dens Park, or rather lack of it, induces in me a disturbing suspicion of the memory.

There are two methods of coming to terms with this. Either Dens Park has shrunk or I have grown. You may find the latter theory more persuasive. I prefer to cling to the former. Because, apart from a belief in the erstwhile grandeur of Dens Park, the other basic pillar of a lifetime's faith is that one day Scotland will win the World Cup.

Dark blue has that effect. But it is not silly to be proud of Scottish football. For a start, take a history lesson. The English may have invented the game, but the Scots civilised it. They made its existence worthwhile. They invented dribbling and passing, which is why their clever little players were brought south to smoking great cradles of the Industrial Revolution in professionalism's infancy. Their purpose was to alter the proportions of brain and brawn, much as a century later the English felt a need to leaven their doggedly instinctive strongarm approach with wily foreigners: from Ossie Ardiles and Arnold Mühren to Eric Cantona, Jürgen Klinsmann and Gianfranco Zola. Their forerunners had been the likes of Hughie Gallacher and Alex James.

The reasons Scotland's products were seldom deemed fit to supply England's needs in the twenty years after Liverpool signed Kenny Dalglish from Celtic are many and complex. Yes, to an extent Scotland had neglected its tradition of footballing culture. As elsewhere, children could take Route One out of boredom through electronics. Emerging talent became a question of numbers, and what Scotland could not overcome was the fact that its population was one-tenth the size of England's. But I still think the setback to our hopes of winning something caused by this barren period is probably temporary. After all, Denmark won the European Championship in 1992 and Denmark has a population only slightly bigger than ours. It is simply a matter of organisation, at which we so excel that the story of the English league championship since the Second World War is substantially one of Scottish management. Sir Matt Busby, Bill Shankly,

Alex Ferguson, George Graham and Kenny Dalglish have all written indelible chapters, as surely would Jock Stein had he been persuaded to leave Celtic for the south in his prime. And now we have Craig Brown, at last receiving the praise he deserves for having maintained a habit of qualifying for World Cups. None of his predecessors delivered the goods with as few players of class. Our pride was ready to go into retirement, I sense, when Brown came along. His is a magnificent achievement. He has kept a dream alive.

What he can never do, of course, is prevent Scots from measuring themselves against the English: an impossible criterion, you might think, but one which provided the overwhelming sustenance of my youth, during which the annual Scotland–England match guaranteed participation in something as gut wrenching as a cup final. I discovered later that it was the game's oldest international fixture. But to us it seemed the only one and since 1876, when it was played for the fifth time, Scotland had been ahead in terms of the number of victories recorded. In our small world, we were champions. I was eight when England won 7–2 at Wembley, unlucky thirteen when they won 9–3, but comfort on those distressing afternoons came from the simplest arithmetic. We still led the series. When I look back, I appreciate it was among the most wonderful examples of big-brother baiting in sport (along with those of Australia and the West Indies in cricket and Wales in rugby union; the English tail does seem to have invited a fair bit of twisting in its time) and it gave us a feeling of privilege, of being special, that even now declines to go away.

The day that dominates the memory was in 1967, when England were the actual world champions and Scotland had a point to make at Wembley. Seldom can eleven players have so precisely articulated what was in the hearts of their supporters. England, with Jack Charlton hobbling hopelessly and substitutes a thing of the future, were at Scotland's mercy. They were beaten 3–2. It could have been more had the Scots, especially Jim Baxter and Denis Law, used their skills to pile on the goals rather than the agony. Baxter, in whose impudence still lies the soul of Scottish football, played keepie-uppie. Law smirked. Much has always been made of Law's disclosure that, a year earlier, he had not been able to bear the thought that England would beat West Germany in the World Cup final and sought refuge from the event on a golf course. But every Scot understood. Social and political domination had made us obsessed with England. On our trips to London, we draped ourselves in tartan embroidered with a chip on the shoulder. We were always in the majority at Wembley because the English cared less. They had bigger fish to fry and I doubt if a single English fan noticed when, ten years ago, shortly before the series was abandoned, their forty-first win put them in front. I noticed. But I was in the press box, trying desperately to be mature and detached.

And succeeding, I like to think. People often find it strange that a football writer should live in England, feel more firmly at home there than in Scotland and yet fail the Tebbit test so dismally that all opponents of the three lions have his sympathy; only the degree varies. Some of those brought up in Scotland are weird this way, others not. What irks me is the occasional inference that I am thereby suspect when reporting England's matches. Of course I am no more so than the majority of my colleagues who are England fans with laptops. When your living depends on honest perception, your commitment to that is total. You put childish feelings in their proper place at the back of your mind. Always. Well, almost always. When Scotland played at Wembley during the European Championship, I was sad that Gary McAllister, such a thoroughly admirable footballer, should have put a crucially timed penalty against David Seaman rather than into the net. But England deserved to win. It was their next match that gave me a personal problem, because they were so brilliant that Holland were four goals down and I heard that, if it stayed that way, Scotland, concurrently leading Switzerland at Villa Park, would qualify for the second stage of an international tournament for the first time. That they would owe it to England was unthinkable, except that I was thinking about it when Patrick Kluivert scored Holland's consolation. And, quite frankly, mine. I did not care to be patronised for the rest of my life. There was a taste of what might have been when, at a party in London that night, well-meaning friends broke off from singing about the damned lions on their sodding shirts to tell me they were sorry Scotland had gone out. I said it was all right. Honestly.

The Tartan Army, as Scotland's travelling fans are somewhat inappropriately known, went home in peace as usual, their reputation intact. No longer are they associated with the boorishness that left parts of London cowering from time to time, before the English became the villains, doing much, much worse to Europe. There is a theory linking the past misbehaviour of Scots in London to English hooliganism in Europe. It is about the destructive effects of an inferiority complex. It is persuasive when, over and over again, you see how unedifying crass chauvinism sits on some English shoulders.

The Scots have learned to take themselves less seriously. They have their own version of Kipling's twin impostors. These are not triumph and disaster but reaching a tournament and leaving it, and treating them just the same is quite easy because they follow each other in such swift succession. Not that the tartan thousands waste a moment when they are there. They began to acquire a sort of ambassadorial status during the 1974 and 1978 World Cups, when England did not qualify and the Scots fans were accepted as different from the English or the same as the rest, depending on how you cared to look at it. In other words, they could drink with the Danes or the Germans, have a laugh, swap shirts, maybe make too much noise but be relied upon to stay out of trouble until things went wrong on the field and they could go home. Football writers tend to avoid fans during tournaments, partly because we are there to work and envious of their freedom, but when I first covered a World Cup in Spain in 1982 it was a joy to be among the Scots.

The night of nights was in Seville, after they had been beaten by Brazil. Four-one. Scotland had made the mistake of taking the lead, through David Narey's 'toe-poke', as we were told Jimmy Hill had preposterously called it on television. But Scotland's sufferings did not alter the mood of the unsegregated crowd and afterwards there was one long carnival. I surveyed it from the crowded terrace of a riverside restaurant, eating seafood and drinking white wine, the latter in such volume that memory of the company remains vague. In fact I recall only Billy McNeill, the captain of Celtic's Lisbon Lions, although my colleague John Moynihan, whose collections of essays, *The Soccer Syndrome* and *Soccer Focus*, are up with the most delightful football writing, must have been there because every June I receive a postcard from some holiday spot with the scrawl: 'Not a patch on the Rio Grande, Seville, I'm afraid.'

What made the night for me was its conclusion. Dawn was breaking, and coffee responsible for a measure of sobriety, when I left the restaurant and encountered something indelibly beautiful. Towards me were staggering a group of about a dozen fans. Though happily mingled, they fell into two categories. Half had smooth skins, shades of coffee. Half were freckled and glowing. Half wore the green and gold of Brazil. Half wore Scotland blue, kilts and tammies. Nothing odd about that; all over the city the fans had got together to sing and dance the small hours away. But the coffee skins were dressed as Scots and the freckles proudly wore Brazil's strip. Did they ever change back into their own clothes, or did a sprinkling of swarthy Rob Roys appear later among the Brazilian crowd who watched their team succumb to Italy in Barcelona? Who knows? But whenever since I have been asked for evidence that football can satisfy the best instincts of humanity I have thought back to that vision in Seville and sighed. It was anything but exceptional. I just think it would have made a lovely poster: the fans' equivalent of the 1970 embrace between Pelé and Bobby Moore.

Scotland played only once in Seville. They met New Zealand and the Soviet Union in Malaga and I was among a group of journalists booked into a hotel at Fuengirola, on the Costa Del Sol, our base for the opening phase. As soon as we arrived I took one look at the swarming tourists and demanded that the agent move me. 'Look,' I said, 'I need a businessman's type of place. We're here to work, for heaven's sake!' I sat on my bags until eventually he cajoled me into the courtesy of inspecting my room. Still nursing righteous indignation, I went with him. It was on the top floor, the fourteenth, where a massive sitting-room led to two double bedrooms, each with bath. In the middle of the sitting-room was a spiral staircase to the roof, where I had my very own swimming pool, bar and barbecue, with views of the shimmering, sail-flecked Mediterranean. 'Right,' I told the agent. 'I'll stay. But don't do this to me again.'

My humour having improved, so did my social life, although it was on a night away from the penthouse party scene that I became a hero. I think it was after the Soviet match, when the method Scotland had devised for knocking themselves out involved a collision between Alan Hansen and Willie Miller which allowed a bystander to run away and beat Alan Rough. At any rate the fans in the bar where I went to relax afterwards were philosophical, not to say pissed out of their minds, and I was halfway to catching up when one of the most arresting figures I have ever seen swaggered through the door. If we had been in a Western movie, the piano would have stopped. He was tall yet almost square, with a body that had clearly been built. His face was tanned and handsome but far too young for a Salvador Dali moustache that, in other circumstances, might have caused me to laugh. He might even have been wearing a cape. But so evil was his sneer, whose menace a few lurking companions were attempting to emulate, that there could be no mistaking whom he intended to be: the Spaniard who blighted our lives. The invitations that duly followed were, to the credit of all but one Scottish subject, ignored. But a simple lad, befuddled, suddenly started to walk towards a battering that would surely have set off general mayhem. To pretend that in a split second I envisaged the headline 'Bar wrecked – brawling Scottish fans no better than English after all!' would be ludicrous, but impulsively I put my arms around the poor wee contender and, in a conveniently positioned ear, whispered the classic sedative: 'Calm down, son, you'd kill him, but he's not worth it.'

The boy went limp, the Spaniard left in frustration and the World Cup passed off without a stain on the Scottish character. Well, that's my claim to fame anyway. I like to think I've done something for the old country.

Four years later, in Mexico, I saw little of Scotland, having become what in national newspapers we rather pretentiously call a 'number one'. If you are based in London, that usually means covering England, which is enjoyable because the space allocated to articles more closely corresponds to the passion expended. But before revelling in the drama of the Hand of God match I did have an opportunity to see Scotland get things right. Or so it seemed. To progress to the knockout stages, they had to beat Uruguay in a Soweto-style suburb of Mexico City known as Neza and when, sixty seconds into the match, a Uruguayan named Batista scythed down Gordon Strachan a quite remarkable show of resolve by the young French referee, Joel Quiniou, apparently eased their task. He sent Batista off. This was before the new FIFA refereeing regime which called for a tough attitude to dangerous tackles; and, in those days, players could expect to give adversaries a first-minute frightener with impunity. Several thoughts went through my mind. Had Quiniou plucked the wrong card from his pocket? Had he, like me, been brought up to believe there was a special relationship between France and Scotland? No, I think he was simply ahead of his time, and it is interesting to note that he stayed around at the top level for many years. But his reduction of Uruguay to ten men, even when they were still smarting from a 6–1 defeat by Denmark in their previous match, failed to break them. Their spoiling tactics – fouls, faking, time-wasting – seemed to mesmerise Scotland and an ungainly miss by Steve Nicol summarised the persistent view that a scoreless draw would be the outcome, which proved accurate. Home again. But again there was satisfaction in having been there, albeit tinged with sadness that the qualification process contained the death of Jock Stein from a heart attack after Davie Cooper's late penalty equaliser in Wales; Alex Ferguson took over for the tournament.

The Scottish FA changed tack thereafter, abandoning big-name management in favour of coaches who had risen through the national youth system: Andy Roxburgh and then Brown, his erstwhile assistant. This made sense. With few players of high quality from which to choose, the knack was to know your resources and blend them. The fans grudgingly accepted a worthy but boring concept and, after Roxburgh's Scotland had set a British record by qualifying for the fifth time in a row, journeyed to Italy to discover that old habits died hard. Roxburgh could hardly have differed more starkly from Ally MacLeod, the showman who led Scotland to Argentina in 1978 and saw them draw with Iran and lose to Peru before signing off with a victory over Holland, the eventual runners-up, that featured Archie Gemmill's sensational goal. Yet twelve years on the pattern was not so different. They lost to Costa Rica and beat Sweden.

Many years ago, before Scotland became practised qualifiers, a friend of mine used to wail: 'Why do we always end up needing to beat Portugal away?' His lament came back to me in Italy when, to stay, we had to beat Brazil and, naturally, lost. But at least the rarity value of Jim Leighton's error illustrated that our goalkeepers were no longer a joke. Two years later Roxburgh set another record by becoming the first Scotland manager to qualify for both a World Cup and a European Championship and, in Sweden, where the European tournament took place, I had the fortune briefly to become a fan again.

A fortune decidedly mixed for, unwittingly, I introduced my girlfriend at the time, Lucy Swann, to the extremes of tournament life. The idea was that she would arrive in Malmo on a Saturday, the eve of England's match against France, watch it, then take a long drive north with me to see Scotland against Germany in Norrkoping the following day. They would be easy days, far from the deadline for a Sunday newspaper (I had escaped from the daily grind). Her England, my Scotland: a perfect combination designed to stimulate Lucy's minimal, largely dutiful, interest in football.

Well, she reached Malmo all right – and walked almost straight into a riot. The local authorities had decided to treat England's fans with kid gloves, laying on entertainment and cheapish beer in a central square. We were having a meal with friends there in a basement restaurant when the manager said we'd have to stay put; there was trouble outside. The Swedes' hospitality had backfired. Perhaps, to paraphrase the FA's one-sided report on the clashes in Rome that were to come five years later, the police had under-reacted. We could hear sirens and smashes. When we emerged, things were quieter but still dangerous. Avoiding every English eye, we hurried to the sanctuary of our hotel and I shall never forget the tears of a bride, her wedding reception ruined.

'This sometimes happens,' I told Lucy. 'I'm sorry it happened to you.' She just kept shaking her head. I promised her Norrkoping would be different and knew that, this time, there truly was no risk. Sure enough, the Scottish fans heard her English accent, sensed the prospect of a conversion, and soon had her giggling helplessly. After the match, during which Scotland's performance was the best I have ever seen from them in defeat (and McAllister, the man I had asked Lucy to watch most closely, marvellous), we hit the town and saw Germans and Scots entwined, teaching each other songs as diligently as the beer would allow. Again she shook her head, but happily. She was enchanted. She had seen the sunny side of football, even if the game was to form but a passing phase of her life.

Lucy is now married to Clem Curtis, lead singer of the Foundations, chart-toppers in the late Sixties with 'Baby Now That I've Found You' and 'Build Me Up Buttercup', and I have no doubt that hobnobbing with the likes of Edwin Starr and Jimmy James (of Vagabonds fame) beats the hell out of fleeing a mob of tattooed tossers in a Malmo square. But I do believe she enjoyed her day and night on tartan territory and cannot help nurturing the thought that, when Scotland do win the World Cup, she will raise a glass and explain to a bemused Clem: 'Oh, it's nothing really. Just some people I used to know.'

we're the famous tartan army

HARRY RITCHIE

Looking back, it's obvious that a key factor was the opening game – catching Brazil on the hop and sneaking a draw when Colin Calderwood kneed the ball in during that last-minute scramble. After Calderwood's second of the tournament – the astonishing free-kick – proved enough to defeat Norway, you could sense that the force was with Scotland. And so it proved when the boys in blue rallied against Morocco to turn the deficit at half-time into a glorious 3–1 victory, Calderwood completing his hat-trick with the thirty-yard bicycle kick that the world's pressmen would unanimously hail as the goal of the tournament. Having progressed beyond the group stage for the first time in six attempts, Scotland breezed through when Calderwood notched up his sixth and seventh goals against . . .

And there the fantasy ends, because although I'm writing this only a couple of weeks after the draw for the World Cup, I can't remember which team Scotland would face if they some-how made it past the group stage.

Which is only sensible. Any Scot who genuinely expects the lads to embark on a long march forward in France has to be unusually silly and newly released from a twenty-year hiberna-tion. Ever since the Argentinian 'campaign' of 1978, when Ally MacLeod demonstrated his unswerving dedication to ensuring national humiliation, misery and despair, Scottish supporters have learned the value of retaining low expectations. Lest there have lurked any danger of us forgetting MacLeod's masterclass in hubris, successive World Cups have provided Scots with regular reminders that Fate can be a fickle mistress and that their team can be traumatically pish.

Scots' hard-won realism about the team's status and prospects stands in marked contrast to our beloved neighbours to the south, where assessment of the English team veers hysterically between an addict's level of self-hatred and an arrogance that Jonathan Aitken would consider unacceptable. (Just for future reference, I'd like to mention at this point that the first report I heard by an English journalist on the World Cup draw included some considered speculation who the other finalist might be. I mean, fucksake . . .)

In a tournament of imponderables, where anything and everything might happen, in what is bound to be a footballing fiesta of turn-ups and shocks and improbable glories, we Scots can benefit from the rare luxury of clairvoyance. I know that, theoretically, events could prove me wrong – and, of course, few things bar the participation of Raith Rovers in a European Superleague would give me greater joy than if my prediction turns out to be wildly inaccurate – but everyone knows what will happen to the Scots in France. The team will probably scrape a point or maybe two, and might, at best and freakish occurrences permitting, win one, draw one, lose one, but even then, Scotland, as everyone knows, will be pipped for second place by Norway or Morocco who will – how could it be otherwise? – have scored one goal more.

Just as certainly, this ill-starred team will be cheered on by thousands of tartaned, kilted fans who will go mental in an ostentatiously well-behaved sort of way and who will bawl themselves hoarse urging Glenn Hoddle to cheer up although he is a sad English bastard with a shite football team. And when, after three games, Scotland's '98 World Cup campaign draws to a close, the Tartan Army will be raucously, defiantly loud and proud in defeat. While the inevitable last-minute own goals and refereeing blunders allow England to survive, preposterously, until the semi-finals (where, of course, they will be knocked out on, all being well, penalties, by, fingers crossed, Germany), we Scots will draw comfort from several reflections – that we're happy just to have been in the competition and to have occupied the same pitch as Brazil (though, admittedly, only that bit of the pitch around our own penalty box), and to have enlivened the tournament with what we will insist to anybody daft enough to listen was a uniquely impassioned and colourful celebration of national pride and identity.

Conveniently ignoring, for the moment, any niggling doubts about this, let's concentrate on what rap artists term the positivity and acknowledge an obvious and wonderful truth – that, in marked contrast to their English colleagues, Scots fans do not have an image problem. Au contraire. Whereas a travelling English fan will assume, correctly, that riot police the world over will buff their kicking boots at the glimpse of a football supporter wearing a Union Jack shawl, a frightening proportion of the Tartan Army's infantrymen actually believe that they only have to do a wee jig and hoist their kilts over their heads to secure drinks on the house and a blow-job from the waitress. A mildly insane assumption, it's true, but the mundane reality is still pretty encouraging, for Scots fans are clearly out to enjoy themselves rather than destroy cities. Hence the joke-shop headgear – just as the Dutch signal they're up for a jolly time by wearing hats that feature rubber axes and Norwegian party-people don their Viking helmets, so the Scots can clamp on their comedy tammies (with amusing carrot dreads) because they're on for a knees-up, not a punch-up. Pissed they may be – in fact, pissed they are obliged to be, constantly, by legal requirement – but the members of the modern Tartan Army are professionally committed to jovial ebullience with alfresco ceilidhs and hands-across-the-water singalongs. Which, it goes without saying, are performed with even greater joviality just after the lads of St George have trashed a ferry or wrecked a plaza.

The Tartan Army's genuine commitment to benevolent partying is also plainly signalled by its repertoire of songs, which retain a reassuringly nostalgic and un-nasty tone, since most of these songs date from the early seventies when singing was something football crowds started to do a lot of. 'Flower of Scotland', copied from rugby internationals in the early eighties, is a relatively recent addition to the few staples, such as 'Bonnie Scotland (We'll Support You Evermore)', 'Scotland (I'd Walk a Million Miles For One of Your Goals' – why the conditional tense?) and, a real period chant this, for match use only, 'Gerrin tae them'. There was one vile ditty unique to Scotland internationals but it has been deleted from the Tartan Army's thin songbook because it was a song for a very special occasion and that occasion no longer exists. I hope and pray I haven't dreamt this, for, according to my memory, the occasion was the traditional display at Hampden by the Ayr Majorettes, a bunch of mostly pre-pubescent girls who, as part of the pre-match entertainment, were required to strut and prance about in skimpy, micro-skirty cheerleaders' kit; when the poor wee things high-stepped their way in front of the vast terrace that was Hampden's Rangers End, they would be serenaded by the Rangers End choir (pop. 26,000) howling out, with such awful ferocity that it transformed that Bread of Heaven tune into an anthem of dark menace:

> *Get it up you.*
> *Get it up you.*
> *Get it up you while you're young.*

(Even as a youth, even in pre-enlightened 1973, I used to

wonder who booked the Ayr Majorettes' annual gig in front of the Rangers End, and why.)

Another significant favourite, exclusive to the Tartan Army, can be traced to the same era, carbon-datable by the tune (of that old British Airways ad about flying the flag) and by the original context (television coverage of Scotland–England matches at Hampden, where the pundit in question spouted to camera from a precarious, temporary gantry while trying to ignore the bricks bouncing off the plastic windows behind him):

We hate Jimmy Hill.
He's a poof.
He's a poof.

A lyric of genius, summing up, with six syllables fewer than a haiku, the iconic loathability of the man and, crucially, his Anglocentric arrogance. In recent years, the song has managed not only to survive Jimmy Hill's waning media career but to prosper. This strange development has seen fancy-goods merchants do a roaring trade in 'Jimmy Hill/He's a poof' flags and the man himself take legal action against the sponsor of the Scottish supporters' homepage on the Internet, where readers were treated to translations of 'We hate Jimmy Hill/He's a poof, He's a poof' in over thirty-five languages, including Mandarin.

So, equipped with the songs, the joke-shop tammies, the commitment to happy-go-lucky partying, and with realistically humble expectations of the team, we Scots prepare to embark on yet another short World Cup campaign, full to the brim with self-delight and self-congratulation. Nor is there too much danger of this changing – one, because Scots are not given to calm, reasonable and possibly critical assessment of any aspect of our collective culture and, two, we can't rely on any outsider telling us some home truths for the simple reason that, to be frank, when it comes to the topics of Scotland, Scots and Scottishness, nobody else can be arsed to have an opinion.

The result is that while the rest of the world ignores us and we busy ourselves with telling each other how great we are as fans, we manage to ignore several basic realities about Scottish football and the very troubling conflicts behind the apparently wonderful, united and coherent Scottish identity – a little scary, yes, we'll grant you that, but – what's your name, pal? Michel? There's a fucking wee drink for you, Michel – good-natured in our kilts and amusing hats, and one hundred per cent of us self-evidently one hundred per cent devoted to the national cause.

Basic reality number one – contrary to our self-promotion, Scots supporters really shouldn't claim to be the world's best/loudest/most passionate – not while there are Brazilians or Argentinians or Jamaicans or Turks or Croats ... Sure, we make a racket and we have a unique brand identity because many of our male fans wear highly patterned skirts, but let's bear in mind that this doesn't give us a monopoly on passion and that a World Cup qualifier managed to instigate a war between Honduras and El Salvador.

Basic reality number two concerns a home truth that is almost never acknowledged in Scotland, not despite but because of its barking obviousness – our team is not, I'm truly sorry to say, a national one. Scotland exists as a separate footballing country on sufferance; if Havelange and his cronies at FIFA had their way, Scotland and the other three home nations would be replaced by one side representing Great Britain, and why not, given that the home nations have a weaker political status than Catalonia or Bavaria? Indeed, the fact that Scots haven't acquired anything like political independence is due, in some measure, to its footballing independence; football acts as an outlet for patriotic passions that would otherwise be diverted into politics, singing about bonnie Scotland having proved much easier than actually doing something about campaigning or voting for one. Just as a successful national team has drawn energy away from political nationalism, an unsuccessful one has wreaked damage on our collective self-esteem, so that a significant factor in the scuppering of the devolution referendum of 1979 was the World Cup shambles of 1978.

Basic reality number three is so evident that even we Scots remain at least residually aware of it – Scottish football is crap. Hence the fact that Craig Brown is being rightly praised as a genius for getting this distinctly unstarry bunch of players into the finals. The problem facing Brown is quite the reverse of the one faced by most of his predecessors who had a lot of talented players at their disposal but no team. The current dearth of great or even good Scottish players can be appreciated by noting how few there are featuring in the top teams in the English Premiership; in the good old days each top English team just had to have at least a trio of key Scottish players but now only Blackburn has that complement while the total number of Scots in the squads of all the other big clubs south of the border has dwindled to three – Steve Clarke who gets an occasional outing for the Chelce, Scott Marshall who gets to play twice a year in the Arsenal firsts and Brian McClair who gets to play in his own testimonials. Anyone who dares to disagree with me on this issue should now try to answer the following question: if Scottish players are so good, why oh why has Craig Brown been driven to Charltonian depths by signing up the chuffed but stunned Matt Elliott, on the grounds that his granny once had a week's holiday in Troon?

The worldwide spending spree of the Old Firm and the bulk buying of unsung Europeans by most other clubs in the Scottish Premier League have failed to make up for this lack of home-grown talent, so that the quality of the domestic game is very poor. How else to explain the extraordinary career of Marco Negri, a striker who enjoyed no more than a reasonable reputation in Serie A but whose move to Rangers has seen him average about five goals a game? How else to explain the abject record of Scottish clubs in European competitions, where Rangers, invincible in Scotland, aspire to mere embarrassment, and where, to take one sorry example from many, Kilmarnock struggled to beat Shelbourne and were then gubbed by Nice, a resolutely average French side? (There is one exception to this ghastly rule of defeats in Latvia and Liechtenstein, and it just happens to be the 1995 UEFA Cup campaign of Raith, who overcame the might of Gotu Itrottarfelag of the Faeroe Islands, saw off Akranes of Iceland and gallantly succumbed, by an eminently respectable 1–4 on aggregate and after taking a 1–0 lead into the interval at the Olympic Stadium, to Bayern Munich, who went on to win the competition after beating every other team at least 10–0 home and away. Just thought this was worth a little mention.)

Who or what can we blame for the dismal standard of Scottish football, for what was once a bubbling, babbling river of talent having turned into a dry track of shingle and rock? One convenient scapegoat is schools football, which went into a tailspin in the eighties just when Scotland's professional coaches were deciding to stamp out flair and skill and to promote the virtues of stamina and work-rate. But I think that another extremely pertinent factor is the glaring failure of just about everyone involved in the Scottish game to come to terms with the new pass-and-move football which requires not only control and skill but patience and intelligence – qualities which, in Scotland, as the most casual viewer of the 'highlights' in Tartan Extra will attest, are conspicuous by their absence.

However, the most obvious culprit of all is never named by the Scottish media because the culprit in this case, and in so many, many other cases, is the Old Firm, and no Scottish newspaper or television programme is going to diss Rangers and Celtic for any reason because that would be to alienate over half of the people buying the paper or watching the telly – although it's as clear as a Duncan Ferguson headbutt that Rangers and Celtic have preferred to buy in foreign talent rather than try to nurture home-grown stars, and that in both clubs young Scots are doomed to pursuing careers wearing squad numbers in the sixties and seventies while the first teams are populated by guys called Henrik and Jonas.

But the decline of their once-vigorous nursery systems is a paltry business compared to the real damage Rangers and Celtic are now doing to Scottish football, damage which the songs and the kilts and the bonhomie of the Tartan Army try too hard to camouflage. Scottish fans may have given every appearance of being united and committed to the cause of the 'national' team but this hides the dire tribalism which has overwhelmed the Scottish game.

Of course, there's nothing new in pointing out that, despite what both clubs claim, Rangers and Celtic were not only founded on a sectarian basis but continue to be funded by sectarianism. Granted, Fergus McCann launched his much-mocked Bhoys against Bigotry initiative and, granted, Rangers have recently managed to sign the odd player from far-flung Catholic countries but both clubs still profit massively from the tribal hatred generated by support for the Old Firm.

You would have thought that the (albeit slowly and unsurely) improving political climate in Northern Ireland would have been reflected in a decline in the hatred between Protestant Rangers and Catholic Celtic. However, impossible though this is to gauge accurately, it does seem that recent years have seen the hostility between the two sets of supporters grow even more hysterical, because Rangers have upped the ante by spending more and more money on imported stars and by going for a record-breaking ten titles in a row. Ten in a row. What, you might think, is the appeal of supporting the equivalent of Manchester United who have to conquer the equivalent of Manchester City (as was), Bury, Oldham and Stockport to win the equivalent of the Greater Manchester League year after year after year? Ah, but that is to reckon without the Rangers fans' Proddie triumphalism, which has always been impervious to everything apart from puffing themselves up and putting the Fenians in their place. 'We are the people,' they sing, and by Christ they mean it. (Just in case any Rangers supporter – or, to use the more evocative term, Hun – accuses me of being a pro-IRA, Sinn Fein-voting, incense-flinging Celtic fan, I'd like to call attention to my resolutely blue-nose surname and – bearing in mind the joke, Q: How do you know ET's a Protestant? A: Because he looks like one – to the pertinent fact that my face resembles a root vegetable. I'd also like to cite a great-uncle who campaigned vigorously and successfully against our kirk holding candlelit services at Christmas, on the grounds that these would necessarily involve the distinctly Papist frippery of candles.)

As the stakes have increased in the past few years, so the two tribes have banged their drums louder and louder and daubed themselves with ever-more garish war-paint. The Billy and Tim identities have developed to the point where they have become near-caricatures of themselves. And here's the rub, because as the nineties have progressed, the two clubs which, more than ever, dominate Scottish football have seen their violently strong identities evolve from being non-Scottish (neither club plays under the Scottish flag, tradition demanding allegiance to the Union Jack or the Irish Tricolour) to becoming, remarkably, anti-Scottish.

Two incidents highlight this peculiar and depressing development. The first happened at the start of this season, when

Hearts fans at Ibrox proclaimed their defiance to the surrounding Rangers support. What provocative song did they choose? 'Stand up if you hate the Huns'? Something not very nice about Andy Goram, maybe? No – they sang 'Flower of Scotland'. As expected, this was answered by a manically fervent rendition of 'God Save the Queen'. Well, it could have been worse, because in the past couple of years, helped a bit by their adoration of Paul Gascoigne, the Rangers fans' staunchly pro-Unionist stance has graduated, preposterously, into a pro-English one. Difficult though it might be to imagine, every fortnight in Glasgow, over 50,000 Scots can be heard bawling out the national anthem, as well as 'Rule Britannia' and – get this – 'Swing low, sweet chariot'.

The second incident I witnessed in 1994, when a very poor Celtic team scraped a 0–0 draw with Raith at Kirkcaldy. An amazingly quiet Celtic support came to life only once that afternoon, at half-time when the tannoy announced that a last-minute drop goal by Rob Andrew had meant England beating Scotland by one point. From the Raith support came a very sporadic and very muted groan – it was Scotland–England and it was a wee shame, but it was, after all, only rugby. But the Celtic supporters burst into wild celebration, revelling in our disappointment on the grounds that we were Scottish, unlike them because they were Irish. It was a tactic intended to sneer and goad, and it fulfilled its function brilliantly – brawls broke out in the ground's one unsegregated stand, and no fucking wonder.

Do these anti-Scottish poses of both Rangers and Celtic fans reflect or even encourage a genuine rejection of Scottishness? It's impossible to say because the research doesn't exist and it's difficult to imagine that any opinion polls or questionnaires would ever be astute enough to deliver reliable answers to that question. At a guess, I'd say that someone called Sean O'Flaherty who has been a season-ticket holder at Parkhead ever since his third year at St Mary-the-Holy-Mother-Full-of-Grace High School would be more likely to feel less Scottish than someone called Fraser Hamilton who has furtive, tingly feelings about Brian Laudrup and the cheekbones of a potato. Fraser might bring himself to root for Gazza in an England shirt, but, push comes to shove, he'll be happily schizophrenic, seeing no problem in singing 'Swing low, sweet chariot' after Negri completes his double hat-trick against Dunfermline, and, the next week, in true Scottish fashion, supporting with a passion whoever it is that's playing England. But what would Fraser do if he were asked to support a Scottish team with five Celtic players and no Gers? Dodgy one. Similarly, who would Sean support if Scotland played the Republic of Ireland? Not a question that mattered in the days when the Republic were dire, before the likes of Ehndy Tahnsend were deemed to be Irish. Now though? Again, that would probably depend on the number of Celtic and Rangers players wearing blue shirts.

Defenders of the Old Firm like to point to the Real–Barcelona nexus in Spain, the big three in Portugal and Holland, and now the big one in England as proof that the shitty imbalance in Scottish football isn't necessarily as bad as people like me like to maintain. Maybe so, maybe not, but the Old Firm is also responsible for prolonging and advertising a wretched tribal bigotry. Plus there's this bizarre business of the crazed and confused loyalties demanded of their supporters to take into account, and once that's been done, it's clear that the Old Firm is a pernicious force, good for one thing, and that's the four lines of a song favoured by Glasgow's third team:

We hate Roman Catholics.
We hate Protestants too.
We hate Sikhs and Muslims.
But Thistle we love you.

By no coincidence, Partick Thistle currently play in a stadium that is one-quarter-developed and, as I write, are facing bankruptcy. The other teams in Glasgow and its hinterland are also struggling to avoid the fate of long-defunct Third Lanark: Clyde have run off to Cumbernauld, Queen's Park are a charming joke, St Mirren are in a mess, and Clydebank's core support has dwindled to two dozen. Their prospects do not look good for the Old Firm casts a big and scary shadow over ever tinier, ever more hapless neutrals. Equally, it requires real, if usually unacknowledged, effort for Scotland's fans to rise to neutrality and ignore the Old Firm's grim, non- and now anti-Scottish agenda. Which explains why the Tartan Army loves to hate the enemy that everyone has in common – the one with the chin.

ronaldo comes from rio

FRANS OOSTERWIJK

PART ONE: 1994-95

1. Grand Paradise

We are introduced in a mixture of Portuguese, Spanish and Dutch. A young face, broad, round, on which the first beard hairs are becoming visible. The teeth caught in the steel frame of a brace, baby down on his head. There is distance in his eyes, but also pleasure, devotion. A drop of sweat hangs from the lobe of his left ear. He is laughing. White spittle at the corners of his mouth.

Grand Paradise 1 is the address where the nightingale has been locked up. Even inside his house the Brazilian has not been left to fend for himself. Philips, sponsor of his club PSV Eindhoven, has given him the latest in modern electronics: laser-disc, telephone, answering machine, fax, television and video. These are the only objects in the house without stickers bearing their names in Dutch.

Ronaldo – bare feet, Michael Jackson cap – clumsily introduces me to Sonia and Nádia. The former is his mother, the latter his girlfriend. Like him, both are dressed for summer. Sonia in a curious white-blue sailor's suit and white Nike shoes as big as clogs. Nádia – red-painted lips, blonde – in an attractive but overtight miniskirt.

Watching TV is Ronaldo's big hobby, the supporter's card says; and that's no lie. Eurosport is showing Brazilian football. Ronaldo almost seems to petrify. With open mouth and a glassy stare he watches the pictures. Sonia and Nádia go to the kitchen to prepare lunch.

The TV-watching continues during the meal. Afterwards Ronaldo produces the video of Bayer Leverkusen–PSV, his first European game. Ronaldo, Sonia, Nádia and Koos Boets, Ronaldo's interpreter, a pater who spent twenty-three years in Brazil, curl up on the sofa.

'Move up, you fat turd,' Ronaldo tells Boets.

'They say all sorts of things to me,' confides the cleric, not in the least put out.

Ronaldo says, 'I phoned my father and said I would score two goals against Bayer. I got three.'

Slowly he sags into the sofa and falls asleep in the arms of his girlfriend. Five minutes later Nádia is out too. I also want to go and lie down somewhere. The food lies heavy on the stomach. The room is like a sauna: 24 degrees, the thermostat says.

I look at Koos Boets, who looks back helplessly. 'He's just come back from training. He's always a little tired then,' he apologises for his pupil's behaviour. Then tenderness gains the upper hand. 'Look at them lying there. But they have already had love troubles. Nádia came to me in the PSV stadium, crying.'

Sonia takes over. She serves black Brazilian coffee and pulls up photograph albums. She has done this before. With short, practised statements, she recounts Ronaldo's life. 'This picture was taken at Valqueire, his first club. He was eight years old. He and his friends had decided that they would all apply to Valqueire together. But Ronaldo left home too late and only arrived when the trial was already over. They could only use him as keeper.'

Then the pictures of his second club, Social Ramos Club, which only played indoor football. Then came São Cristóvão. 'Ronaldo didn't really want to go there at all. His favourite club was always Flamengo. He had a trial there when he was thirteen, but he was turned down. We lived three quarters of an hour away from the city centre and Flamengo didn't want to pay for the daily bus rides. Everyone now thinks that was an absolute blunder.'

Sonia didn't see much in her son's football ambitions. She wanted him to study instead. 'Not because I don't like football, but because it's a trap. A brother of mine, Pipíco, played for Fluminense and later in Venezuela and Colombia. Now he can barely keep his head above water.'

Her face has gone a deep shade of red. Clearly this is a favourite topic.

'From the moment Ronaldo joined São Cristóvão, in 1990, there was nothing to be done with him. He played truant so much that I would take him to school myself and stay for hours to make sure he didn't run away. But in the break he would often get away anyway and leave me standing by the door.'

At the end of that year Ronaldo didn't go to school anymore at all. Seven years of primary school (of the total of eight) – that is what he has acquired of reading, writing and maths.

Now, in the knowledge that her son has become a phenomenon, Sonia is more tender about his educational past. 'I still have a couple of his old school notebooks,' she smiles. 'He only wrote down the names of famous footballers, and line-ups.'

There is even pride. Because his talent comes from his mother's side, of course. After all, her brother was a pro.

The picture drawn by his mother requires some revision, thinks Ronaldo when he wakes up. 'I didn't always want to be a footballer,' he says irritably. 'I used to want to be a musician.' He also never said, as his mother claims he did, 'that he is on earth to score'; he isn't that high-flown. 'But I do have a sense of predestination. That this is my profession, my role in life: to play football and entertain others.'

Like Baggio, I ask, who once compared himself with Michelangelo and Leonardo da Vinci?

'With who?' Ronaldo asks. 'Never heard of them.'

Outside football his general knowledge is minimal, Koos Boets willingly adds.

But his footballing ambitions are large. Ronaldo wants to be a bit of Pelé, a bit of Garrincha. Pelé for his goals and his career after football, Garrincha for his moves. 'I saw TV pictures of him playing at the 1958 World Cup. Garrincha was dribbling when suddenly, with his marker chasing him, he ran away from the ball and let one of his team-mates pick it up. Such a crazy sight, so brilliant.'

TV-watching, driving lessons, training, Dutch lessons, phone calls, a game of tennis with a PSV team-mate – Ronaldo doesn't do anything else. An adolescent in heaven. 'Oh yes, answering fan mail, I do that too.'

On the cupboard lies an enormous plastic bag full of airmail envelopes, ready to be sent to Brazil. In Holland footballers only answer their fan mail if a stamp has been enclosed. Ronaldo is unaware of this golden rule. 'So far I've sent off 2,000 letters with signed photographs, including 700 to Brazil at Fl 1.60 each.' Mentally he calculates what this has cost him. 'Fifteen hundred guilders [almost £500],' he says. Peanuts, compared with the phone bill.

For the second time he leaves us alone. Together with Nádia he disappears to his room. There is laughter, scuffling, then silence.

Automatically his mother resumes the conversation. With a degree of pathos Sonia talks about the cold life in Holland. Everything frightens her. The language that she can't understand, the big, tall people, the cold, the misery of Eindhoven. But she's not sad. 'I cook, I wash, I have a function,' she says with great dignity. 'Sometimes I'm a little quiet. But Ronaldo always spots that very quickly. Then he does the craziest things to cheer me up. Wrestling, he'll chase after me. Or he'll have bought a fake toy, a spider or something, and try to frighten me. Or he suddenly puts that big bear on the toilet or gets his bike and cycles through the room and sings and shouts. Just to distract me.'

Sometimes the roles are reversed. 'If he hasn't scored, he comes home utterly frustrated. Then you have to be very careful with him, then we make the pace.'

Koos Boets is full of sympathy for the Brazilian colony in Great Paradise. 'Such sweet, brave people. Strong boy, that Ronaldo, a bit shy. And terribly playful, he just can't concentrate. That's why the Dutch lessons are going so badly.'

About Ronaldo's footballing ability Boets has no opinion. He hasn't seen a match yet. PSV couldn't run to a season ticket.

2. São Cristóvão

São Cristóvão was once a club that could trouble Rio's great powers, Flamengo, Vasco da Gama, Fluminense and Botafogo. In 1926 it was state champion and chief supplier to the national team.

But São Cristóvão has followed its neighbourhood downwards. A club of the poor for the poor, kept alive by love and the favours of the odd mycaenas or sponsor. The entrance still has something of the old glory: a marvellous plaque bearing the legend, 'São Cristóvão Football Club'. Beside it, the club's equally beautiful black-and-white coat of arms.

Cement stairs lead past the canteen and the trophy room. When you reach the third floor you think that this can't be the right place. The walls become even more paintless and beat-up. But then a door sweeps open and there, beneath a photo of Ronaldo, sits Ary Ferreira de Sá, manager of São Cristóvão, all warmth and heartiness.

Ary doesn't have a fax or a photocopier. But he does have beer, a fridge full. As he pours it he swears and rails at everyone and everything. At Ronaldo, who has so much luck in his life, and doesn't have the decency to look up his old club. At Martins and Pitta, Ronaldo's managers, shrewd calculators who have cheated him of his best player. At his own president, the idiot, who let Ronaldo go for a couple of thousand dollars.

There is another guest: Alírio José de Carvalho, chairman of the indoor football club Social Ramos, which Ronaldo joined at age twelve.

'An average player,' was Alírio's initial assessment of Ronaldo. 'What was special was his attitude. It was as if he came from the moon. Nothing bothered him, nothing and nobody could impress him.'

Alírio passed four thirteen- and fourteen-year-old boys on to Ferreira: Ronaldo, Alexandre Calango, Zé Carlos and his own son Leonardo. On 12 August 1990 Ronaldo played his first match for São Cristóvão. He scored three times, but Ary wasn't very impressed. 'He was so wooden, so unelegant. He and the ball stumbled through everything, by luck it seemed. Calango, who was playing next to him up front, pleased me more.'

But the more Ronaldo scored, the more Alírio and Ary pandered to him. Food, shoes, bus tickets – they gave him everything. Paid for out of their own pockets or from the club till. Nothing could be expected from Ronaldo's parents. 'His mother went out every evening and came home early in the morning,' sneers Ary. 'Often Ronaldo turned up late for matches. His mother hadn't woken him. So before important matches he often stayed with me. His father never showed himself here either. In all the time he played for us, I saw his father two, three times. It sounds harsh, but the biggest blessing in his career was his parents' divorce.'

In 1993, when Ronaldo was playing for Cruzeiro and

stunning the nation, Ary was suddenly visited by a stream of journalists who couldn't believe that the player was only sixteen. 'That stung me. As if we'd messed about with his player's pass.' In a way Ary can understand it. Between the ages of fifteen and sixteen Ronaldo metamorphosed from an underfed stringbean into a muscular athlete. 'Ronaldo ate his way to the top, you could say.'

At São Cristóvão there is no sauna, bubble bath or fitness room. The showers do produce water, a miserable brown drip, and that counts for a lot.

'Such misery, huh?' Zé Carlos sympathises with me. He crosses himself at the two statues of the Virgin Mary in the middle of the changing room. 'I'll praise the day that I can leave here.'

One by one Zé Carlos has seen all his friends leave: Ronaldo and Calango to Cruzeiro, Leonardo to Vasco. Only he is still at São Cristóvão. There isn't much demand for goalkeepers. He earns $50 a month, his position as first-choice keeper is unthreatened; Carlos likes to moan about the club, but in fact he enjoys himself; his complaints are the cynicism of someone who only wants things to get better. São Cristóvão is his home, he knows everyone; from the shoeshine boys who watch the training to the drunkards who come here to sleep off their intoxication and then pour beer down themselves again.

Zé Carlos hurries upstairs, where Leonardo and Calango are waiting. The three haven't seen each other for a year. The greeting is hearty and loud. The way boys of eighteen, nineteen do it. With slaps on shoulders and prods on bodies. Zé Carlos is big and tall; Calango and Leonardo small and compact. They all have the same stringy, hard footballer's body as Ronaldo; a body that reveals a lifetime of training.

Leonardo, who bites his nails, still plays junior football at

Vasco da Gama. He earns $50 a month plus a contribution towards bus costs. Work hard for another year, and then he'll get a professional contract. He hopes.

'In terms of ability I am closer to Ronaldo than the difference in salary suggests,' he says cleverly.

Calango, open laugh, round face, saw his dream come true in 1994. He was invited for a trial at his favourite club, Fluminense. But when he injured his knee, Fluminense lost interest. Now he sits at home, waiting for the liberating phone call from Martins and Pitta, his agents. In his sombre moments he thinks that 'it' is over, that he has had his only chance.

Friendship too has a hierarchy: Ronaldo's best friend is Calango, the three agree. It was with him that he first climbed the steps to the giant statue of Christ that looks out over Rio. With him he made his first journey in the *téléférique* to the Sugar Mountain. 'Ronaldo and I talked about everything together,' Calango says. 'His parents are divorced too, and he missed his father just as much as I did mine.'

Calango can easily understand why he hasn't heard from his friend for so long. 'He'll be too busy to think about us. Just think what he has to do! Play, train, adjust, live in a new country. Brave, that he can manage all that.'

Zé Carlos: 'It wouldn't hurt him to call just once. But that will come. I'm convinced of it.'

Only Leonardo has his doubts: 'I can't understand that he has been able to forget us so quickly.'

Besides their talent Ronaldo, Calango, Leonardo and Zé Carlos have their background in common. Fathers who work in a garage, as a salesman in an electronics shop or worker on the assembly line. Mothers who sell ice creams, run a fruit stall or cut hair.

Their boyhood memories are happy, free of conflict. City rats, they were. Always on the street, playing football. No messing with drugs, although there was a dealer at every party. No theft – they were too cowardly for that, and also too crazy about football.

'Towel fights in the changing room, throwing stones at dogs and cats,' says Zé Carlos. 'Did you know that Ronaldo is great at imitating queers? And he's a fantastic goalkeeper.'

Calango: 'After practice we often spent whole afternoons in his mother's ice cream salon. Or we went fishing, or to the beach; swimming, surfing a little.'

And of course chasing girls.

Leonardo: 'Except Ronaldo. Because of his teeth. They were so crooked that he could hardly close his mouth. That was the first thing he did when he had money: get braces.'

Calango: 'That's why parties with Ronaldo always ended with football. He just couldn't find a girl.'

How good is their friend as a footballer?

Leonardo sticks to his earlier view: Ronaldo is no better than he. If he had had the same chances, he would have come as far. 'Ronaldo is a dribbler, he's lazy,' he says contemptuously. 'He'll never run to win the ball. The ball has to come to him. He's still like that. He just gets more passes now than he used to.'

'You're jealous, Leonardo,' Zé Carlos chastises him. 'Ronaldo is the best. You could see it coming. He used to stand out.'

Calango doesn't commit himself. 'When we were about six, I was definitely better than him. Everyone says so, so it must be true. Now he's taken a lead. He's riper, more experienced.'

'*Sí, sí*, Ronaldo, marvellous player.'

All day Váldir, the ageing concierge, has been sitting in his chair by the gate. Now, late in the afternoon, his work starts. He sprays the field with a garden hose. He is wearing trainers and white shorts. Silver-grey hair all over his body. Like scales.

Did anybody tell me about that one goal? My, my, that was

something. 'The keeper is bouncing the ball, but he doesn't know that Ronaldo is right behind him. Suddenly the boy appears, takes the ball from the keeper, turns him and puts the ball in the net. It was repeated on TV for weeks.'

But you know who was really a player? Garrincha! And immediately the tales roll out. How Váldir lived next door to him for years and enjoyed his parties and barbecues. Friends, drink: wagon-loads full. Until he fell ill and no one came to visit him anymore. That's how Garrincha died. Lonely and deserted, ripped off by his friends. 'But at least he had been the best in the world. I am disintegrating too, but I don't have that consolation.'

3. Nada especial

His laugh fills the hearts of the sombre with hope. A marvellous laugh which melts away all buts, if-thens and asides. Ronaldo laughs easily, at his own jokes or those of others.

There is more in him that wins me over. The care with which he brings me glasses of cola; the way he gives me a place at meals as if that spoke for itself; the earnestness with which he leads me to the big glass table in the kitchen, where we go to have a 'real' talk. The clumsiness with which he escapes difficult questions or situations. When his mother says that 'Ronaldo is on earth to score' he gets angry but then immediately uses exactly the same phrase. When I tell him that his friends wonder why they never hear from him, he shrugs. 'I have only one friend, and that's Nádia,' he says, looking stubbornly ahead. Instantly he corrects himself. I mustn't think that he has forgotten Zé Carlos and Calango. But now is not the time to live in the past. Moreover, he never writes, to nobody.

In Holland he is an alien without a cultural hinterland. Yet he has adjusted terrifically well to the profile of the Dutch professional footballer. Like his colleagues he moves easily in comfort and luxury, and his wardrobe grows by the day. In his spare time, too, he conforms to the profession as it is experienced here. He listens to music (from pop to reggae; no samba), plays tennis, watches Eurosport or a fight movie on video. Most footballers read the newspaper as well as *Voetbal International* – Ronaldo reads nothing. And he doesn't have a dog or children.

He is special only as a player.

Because of his physical strength. Ronaldo has the body of a twenty-five-year-old.

Because of his nerve. He doesn't seem to worry. After the match, you can't tell from his demeanour whether he has scored no goals or three.

His sportsmanship. Ronaldo seldom commits fouls and never protests against refereeing decisions.

Because of his calmness, his introversion. Ronaldo never shouts. Not in the match, not at practice, not at home.

His minimal work at practice. Ronaldo is not a training animal, a quality he shares with all great footballers. At PSV he is the only one who never does weight training.

The unconcern with which he deals with coaches and team-mates, who want to force him into a structure that isn't his. He doesn't talk back, doesn't argue. He laughs, shakes his head. It can mean anything. From, 'OK, I'll do my best' to 'Talk all you want'.

The fact that he is learning Dutch at entirely his own pace. There is something heroic in his refusal to let anyone or anything fire him up. The flipside, that he sometimes lives inside an autistic vacuum, he accepts.

His loyalty. Never does he suggest that he would rather be at Ajax. Never does he say anything negative about PSV or a team-mate.

It is all these characteristics that impress me. You don't expect so much calm and maturity in a boy of eighteen. When I ask where he gets his self-confidence, he looks at me in wonderment, frowns, and searches for answers that will please me.

During one of my visits he happens to show me a video clip by the Brazilian rap group Gabriel O Pensador. This clip says more, I feel, than Ronaldo can.

The song is called *Nada especial*, 'Nothing special', and describes a ride through Rio on the number 175 bus; Ronaldo plays the conductor. At every catastrophe the rappers pass on the way, the bus stops and they give a commentary. Laconic and sardonic. Robbery and murder in broad daylight, drug dealers on every street corner, whores on the beach, bizarre religious sects, floods that stop the traffic: this is Rio. *Nada especial!* Unconcerned, cocky, Ronaldo looks into the camera. The title says it all. If you come from Rio, you can take on the world. Nobody can sell this boy a dud.

Is this just romantic psychology? I wonder later. Isn't a footballer's secret to be found on the pitch?

4. Porto Alegre

It's 21 December, the middle of summer, and the Brazilian team is 'doing' the provinces. Manager Zagalo has been able to call up the entire world championship team for the match against Yugoslavia.

Amid all the bustle and noise Ronaldo is a beacon of peace. He scuttles up and down a corridor between the hotel reception and the bar. Every journalist who grabs him for an interview is granted an audience.

He speaks to them in a stoic, almost aristocratic manner. Not an ice man who considers carefully, but not everybody's friend either. Gracious in his movements. His eyes ahead, his back straight. As I know him from Eindhoven. At most he is a little more exuberant here. Here he doesn't weigh every word on a set of scales. Here, in his own language, he can play with the situation. And the journalists write what they were going to anyway.

Only when he is approached by one of the Lolitas who occasionally seem to emerge out of nowhere, does he seem thrown. Then he becomes an adolescent with a stupid smile and greedy eyes who would love to hurl himself into an amorous adventure, but is held back by his own shyness and the watchful eyes of others. He does have taste: unerringly he separates the real goddesses from the apparitions.

Among the Brazilian journalists Ronaldo is the favourite subject of conversation. It was with surprise that they saw him enter the hotel yesterday: dressed in a yellow shirt, yellow jacket and yellow tie. Very different from the Ronaldo they remember from his time at Cruzeiro, the Ronaldo who went about in tracksuit or jeans.

What surprised them most was his earring. 'In Holland everyone wears them,' Ronaldo had explained.

Eldio Macedo, right-hand man of Renato Marsiglia, the famous Brazilian referee, comes to greet me with a thumbs-up. Macedo has the most beautiful coffee colour I have ever seen. His head is as round as a football, with a woollen roof of grey African hair. 'Hello, how are you?' he says in English, with an enormous toothpaste smile. 'Have a drink. Relax, enjoy. Enjoy is most important matter in life.'

Tripping over the pram with which the wife of Dunga (who lives in Porto Alegre) has made her entrée, he drags me over to Ronaldo, who is standing in reception sorting a small pile of fanmail and simultaneously accepting a red rose from a teenie bopper aged about fourteen. We greet each other, but I am defeated by the competition from three girls. When Ronaldo joins them at a table he forgets the rose. It is carried after him by Macedo, who, most attentively, has put it in a glass of water.

A little later, with a courtly gesture, Ronaldo hands the rose to a lady of considerably greater sexual ripeness than the original donor.

Two tables down Dunga, the Brazilian captain, at the time playing in Germany for Stuttgart, is conversing in broken German with two elderly German tourists. Yesterday I saw him and Ronaldo at the bar together, teasing each other about the countries they play in. Ronaldo acting the good Dutchman, Dunga the bad German. *Dummkopf! Klootzak!*

Dunga is one of the few players in the Brazilian squad with a high school education. His father has a decent civil servant's job in the provincial government of Rio del Sul, his mother (and now his sister too) is headmistress of a *lyceum*. That background is why he is a father figure to many of his team-mates.

His youngest pupil is Ronaldo, who has brought a considerable problem upon himself: he has shown his talent at much too early an age. 'Now everyone expects him to play brilliantly in every match,' Dunga says. Only in the Brazilian team is Ronaldo given time. 'He sees me, Branco, Romário, Bebeto as big brothers, and himself as the little boy who has it all to learn. But he is convinced that he has a great career ahead of him. That there will come a day when he is as important to the others in the team as the others are to him.'

Ronaldo has another guardian angel in the Brazilian team: Márcio Santos, the granite defender. Santos' performance at the World Cup in the States won him a transfer to Fiorentina. And he may get more than that. The chairman of Fiorentina, the film producer Cecchi Gori, has promised to introduce him to Sharon Stone. But only if Santos scores seven times this season.

'So far I have scored twice, but I think Gori will introduce me to her if we just qualify for European football. And I shall receive her with open arms.'

If you hurt Ronaldo, you hurt Santos. The dark athlete

responds indignantly to the rumour current among journalists that Ronaldo did not come on during the last World Cup final because he was shaking with nerves in the dug-out.

So many pockets were picked and cars broken into around the stadium at yesterday's practice, that today the police have refused to admit spectators. But half an hour after training starts, the barricades are removed and hordes of schoolchildren swarm onto the stands.

They have missed the best bit: Ronaldo taking gym lessons from the running coach. The exercise is simple, but Ronaldo cannot master it. He has to throw the ball from beneath his legs over his back, and then, when the ball lands in front of his nose, to start a short dribble. He just can't do it. The ball bounces off his backside or ends up somewhere behind him. Ronaldo is made to look stupid. Jeering, the other players imitate his incompetence.

He takes revenge at the closing kickaround. It's two-touch. Ronaldo is phenomenal. He doesn't score, but every ball is right. He sees the free man, moves the game along.

5. The trickle-down effect

Success in Brazil is something you share with your family. It spreads like an oil stain, and starts with moving house. When Ronaldo became a sensation at Cruzeiro, he made his first purchase: a house in São Cristóvão. For his mother, his brother, his sister and himself.

When he moved to PSV it was his father and brother's turn. Nelinho, the brother, was treated to a flat on Copacabana, and his father to one on Ipanema. Bunkers for the middle classes, closely guarded.

For himself Ronaldo bought a flat on the Avenida Sernambetiba, the fifteen-mile long boulevard by the Barra da Tijuca beach south of Rio. A dorado for investors and speculators, Ronaldo says. Romário lives there too. Looking up from the beach you see a giant *favela* that almost reaches to the clouds, which houses an estimated half a million people. Jacarazinho, points Ronaldo, where Romário grew up.

With waving hands Nelio Luiz Nazário de Lima clears the cigarette smoke. He looks as if he is smoking two, three at a time. Fag-ends balance on the edge of the table, others lie in the ashtrays between the piles of paper, photos, bank statements, envelopes, notebooks, pencils, pens and paperclips.

Ronaldo's father is a tormented man. So many worries, and then having to clear up all sorts of misunderstandings as well. 'Ronaldo's talent comes from me, not from Sonia's brother. From the age of five he ran after me when I was playing for the neighbourhood or the works team. Incidentally, I could have been a pro myself. Bangu, Madureira, Portuguesa, they all wanted me. But I preferred to play with my friends. And still: I play every Saturday. With number 9, just like Ronaldo.'

What they said at São Cristóvão, that he never came to watch, isn't true either. 'I was always there. At least when he started playing on the field. I was never interested in indoor football.'

Small, thin legs: you wouldn't have thought that he was Ronaldo's father. 'Physically we don't look alike. Ronaldo had a better childhood than I did.' But there is something else that Nelio did pass on to his son: calm, balance, intelligence. 'From early on I taught Ronaldo the importance of mental strength.'

It is difficult to approach Nelio without prejudice. Thanks to Ronaldo he at last lives in Ipanema, as he always wanted to. A hundred yards from the beach, in the shadow of restaurants, shops and trees. Away from Bento Ribeiro, where the poor live. It doesn't worry Nelio. Of course he profits from his son. But what's wrong with that? Can't he be lucky for a change?

'Nice flat, isn't it?' he says, proud as a peacock. 'Did you see that porter with the gun? If I want to, I can call room service just like that.'

The flat is in Ronaldo's name. His son also takes care of the daily upkeep. For the moment, that is. 'I've always been able to look after myself, but not just now. Been a bit stubborn. With Ronaldo's help I set up an estate agency, but it went bankrupt.'

Nelio has nothing to hide. Formality is not his style. A woman comes in; messes around a bit in the bedroom, then emerges in different clothes and leaves. Nelio doesn't even look. During our conversation he gets four or five phone calls. 'All women who are chasing me,' he says. A joke or for real – I don't get the time to decide. 'Do you think that in Eindhoven I'd have a chance of a blonde girlfriend?' he asks.

If they knew that you were Ronaldo's father, you probably would, I reply.

'No, I don't want it like that. I mean normally.'

You are a little small. That's not to your advantage.

'There are small blonde women, aren't there?'

A PSV shirt hangs over a chair. 'PSV is getting a new sponsor next year,' I say. 'Nike instead of Adidas.'

Terror grips his heart. 'But Philips is still there, isn't it?'

'Do you know who Ronaldo was named after?' he asks as I leave. 'After the doctor who closed off Sonia's tubes after his birth. Ha, ha. Doctor Ronaldo, his name was.'

6. Young Hamlet

As we stumble over rocks and small slopes towards the sea below us, Ronaldo suddenly stands still. He spreads his hands to heaven and says in priestly tones, 'Brazil is paradise.'

We are thirty-five miles south of Rio, at one of the pearly beaches on the way to São Paulo.

Poetry, ballet, the beauty of movement are the images that Gregory Rood, the New Zealand director, wants for his documentary. Yesterday he filmed a juggling Romário. Today it's Ronaldo's turn, 'the young magician waiting in the wings to play Hamlet,' as Rood phrases it. Then he will continue to Nigeria and Europe. If you are looking for beauty you cannot go far enough, Rood believes.

Like a king Rood leads the fifteen-man crew to the edge of the water, where the first pictures will be shot. Like bearers on a jungle expedition, almost collapsing under the weight of cameras and recorders, they follow him. Most are British, walking in the colonial outfit that seems to have been given them with their genes: tropical helmets with cloths waving behind, and khaki shorts. Their legs are white as milk bottles, and no one dares take off his shirt.

Ronaldo is in the mood. No trace of nerves.

First some shots of him emerging from the waves, Rood decides.

Two hours later: Ronaldo's teeth are chattering from the cold. He has jumped up from the sea at least twenty times and is so exhausted that he can hardly stand anymore. Rood is a perfectionist. Either the wave isn't high enough, or Ronaldo jumps too early or too late. 'One more please,' he commands in English, with a steely smile.

Then Ronaldo is made to juggle the ball. Again he is called upon for a skill he does not possess, and again he fails. The balls glide off his feet.

For a long time Rood, 20 kilograms overweight and long artistic hair over his shoulders, controls himself. He tries to win Ronaldo's favour through flattery. Every ball swept up with shoulder or heel earns hysterical applause. 'Oh, lovely, beautiful.' Ronaldo is embarrassed. Ovations for achievements that any street footballer could better are an insult.

Then Rood's fort of civilisation is overcome by his perfectionism. He walks up to Ronaldo and demonstrates elaborately and exaggeratedly what he expects. With his hand he moves the ball to foot, head, shoulder. 'Celebrating football, you know.' He sprinkles the dried-out Ronaldo with water and walks back. 'Another one,' he snarls. The sudden anger has its effect. Ronaldo at last shows the trick expected of him. Ball in his neck, dropped dead into the side of his knee. Down along his shin, and flicked back up with his foot.

On the way back Ronaldo can't stop talking. Rood is a fatso who has probably never touched a ball himself, the organisation was shit and he's never going to swim again. Every time he ran out of the water he stepped on a piece of plastic or wood; thought that it was an animal or something, and he doesn't like animals.

7. Divide and rule

With iron regularity Ronaldo scores his goals. On the way to the target he set himself at the start of the league season: thirty goals. His goals are unpreventable and perfect, as if realised in the only way possible. His rushes and moves have the same quality. Ronaldo has a sixth sense for the quickest route. He doesn't have Romário's skill and suppleness, but he can turn away from every opponent with ultra-short motions. And he has what cyclists call the third acceleration: the sprint in the sprint, with which he can suddenly shake off two or three men.

Brilliant ideas occur to him. Like against NEC, when he plucked a goal-kick out of the air and in one move lobbed it onto the crossbar.

Ronaldo is enthusiastic about Dick Advocaat, PSV's coach. 'He is pleased with me, and I am with him,' he says plainly. Ronaldo is not a man for hollow phrases. For Advocaat he has sworn off Coca-Cola and potatoes, he says proudly.

He tells me he finds Nádia's endless talk about marriage annoying. 'Annoying, annoying,' she shouts, affronted. 'You can't keep away from me. You're like chewing gum. So why don't you want to marry me?' When Ronaldo, drawn to her as if by a magnet, calms her down with kisses, Koos Boets and Vampeta, PSV's other Brazilian, look the other way in embarrassment. They are fed up with the love doves.

Ronaldo takes me to the garage and shows me his newest possession: a Chrysler Cherokee. At snail's pace he drives me to the station. He takes a curve with painful accuracy, performs every movement slowly and with complete concentration. 'How do you think I drive?'

8. To Milan

On a day off, Ronaldo accepts the invitation of the football agent Giovanni Branchini to take a look in Milan.

This means nothing, argues PSV's general manager, Frank Arnesen. 'He's been to London, Brussels and Paris. This time he wanted to go to Italy. It's the kind of trip players often make. I did it too when I was a player: a weekend off and away you go. Marvellous.'

Ronaldo is not a man to draw up smokescreens. He went to Milan because he expects that one day he will play there, he says upon return. He refuses to say when that will be. 'We didn't look for a house, anyway,' he jokes.

Branchini took them to the cathedral, the Scala theatre, the San Siro stadium. They also shopped extensively. Nádia produces the photographs as evidence. There they are: Nádia and Ronaldo at the cathedral, Nádia and Ronaldo at the Armani and Moschino shops, Nádia and Ronaldo at a hotel covered with chandeliers, Nádia and Ronaldo seated at table with Branchini.

Two things strike me. Firstly, they must have changed clothes five or six times that day. Secondly: the look in their eyes. Nothing can awe Nádia and Ronaldo.

At the end of the season Ronaldo leaves Eindhoven before Nádia. She drives him to the airport. An exuberant Vampeta is there too. Arnesen has told him that he can rejoin the PSV squad next season; he is beside himself with joy. I don't tell him what Advocaat told me: that Vampeta definitely won't get a place in the team, that he can't see what Kees Rijvers, who scouted him, saw in the boy.

It is striking how good Ronaldo looks. Strong, in full glory. The one year in Holland has made him more mature. Calmer, more sure of himself, more business-like. A lace on one of his Nikes is undone. When I make a joke about the poor quality of the shoes, he says laughing: 'Undone laces but a good contract.' No doubt about it: this guy knows how the world works. A little longer and the boy from the videoclip will be gone forever.

I tell him that I met Romário in Rio. He leaps up. Did I see him play? Is he badly injured? Did I know that Ana Paula, his new girlfriend, is the assistant in Xuxa's children's programmes?

He would like a career like Romário's, he bursts out. Money, fame in Europe. Win the World Cup with Brazil. Then, at the end of his career, 'when I'm thirty-five or so', return to Rio and spend his last years with Flamengo. Just like Romário, just like Zico.

PART TWO: 1997-98

9. Barcelona

When practice ends Ronaldo is surrounded by a wood of cameras, microphones and notebooks. While he answers patiently, his eyes search and spy for a gap to escape the throng. Suddenly he is gone: as if he possesses a sixth sense for escape routes that nobody else notices.

Only Aloysio, his housemate and bodyguard, a gigantic black man with the body of George Foreman, cannot be fooled. With a towel he wipes a few drops of sweat from the head of the young master on the way to the changing room. A little later Aloysio waits silently and sombrely by the changing room door, sunk into a white leather chair that can only just accommodate a man of his proportions.

'Come to Barcelona, we'll go for a meal,' Ronaldo had said to me two weeks before, at the UEFA Cup final against Paris Saint Germain. Something in Aloysio's posture tells me that this is not for today.

Five minutes later Jaime Teres, the Barcelona press officer, tells me that I have been granted an audience. He leads me to Ronaldo, who makes his apologies. He has absolutely no free time. All he can do is permit my presence at a TV interview he is about to give to CNN.

Ronaldo sits relaxed in the chair, ready for the work he has to do. In Holland two years ago, every interview was torture for him. That shyness is gone. In Spain he has become a professional football-question-answerer: civilised, patient and polite. But he is not and never will be a charismatic.

Football is only news for CNN if it's about the best player in the world. So that is how Ronaldo is introduced. Then two questions follow at once: are you better than Pelé? What do you think of Maradona?

Ronaldo must have responded to these comparisons hundreds of times, but he still manages to look pleased and surprised.

'It is a great honour for me to be compared with Pelé,' he says in hesitant but flawless Spanish. 'But I am only at the beginning.'

Maradona, whom he has often seen on TV, is an example to him.

But things ended badly with the Argentinian, says the CNN interviewer insinuatingly.

'I can't talk about the Maradona off the field,' says Ronaldo carefully. 'A lot of stories are told about him, I wouldn't know which ones to believe.'

Come, come, encourages the CNN man. Everyone knows that Maradona was brought down by drugs.

'We can all learn from what has happened to Maradona,' Ronaldo says diplomatically. 'There are many bad people in football who only want to use you. But I have a strong character, I know who to associate with and who not to.'

With whom does he feel the most affinity, Pelé or Maradona?

'With Zico,' says Ronaldo, 'my only idol. But I'm not like him. Nor like Pelé or Maradona.'

Asked about the characteristics of his style, he shrugs his shoulders in surprise. As if he was requested to explain how he breathes. 'I do what comes to me,' he says vaguely. 'Dare something, risk something, show the people something special. Apart from that I don't think about it.'

To play simply, you have to be a great footballer, nods the interviewer, and he pulls an understanding face. '¿Qué?' The question has to be repeated before Ronaldo finally grasps the essence. 'Sí, sí,' he says.

'How did you get such a strong body?' the interviewer tries. Must have done a lot of weight training? 'Not at all,' says Ronaldo, for the first time with something like emotion in his voice. 'My strength comes naturally to me. If you saw my older brother, you would understand what I mean.'

When he tries to stand up the producer stops him. The interview isn't finished yet, he says. They still have to shoot some close-ups of the interviewer. While he gently pushes Ronaldo back into his chair, he explains what is expected of him. The interviewer will ask all the questions again, and Ronaldo just has to look in his direction.

A dark cloud crosses the face of the Brazilian hero, the corners of his mouth droop. 'Why didn't you come with two cameras?' he rightly asks. He endures the affliction without complaint, but he doesn't laugh anymore.

Ronaldo's girlfriend, the Brazilian model Susana Werner, has spent some time with an interior designer shaping their house on the Mediterranean coast entirely to their tastes. This suggests to many Barcelona watchers that he will stay with the club. But others say he is going to Inter Milan. The Italian fashion designer Valentino is already said to have offered his girlfriend a job.

Barcelona has offered Susana, a regular in the Fluminense women's first team, a place in its side.

10. The goal against Santiago de Compostela
There may come a time when Ronaldo curses the goal that he scored on 18 November 1996 against Santiago de Compostela. Not for the goal itself, but for what it brought about. Since that goal his life has been tied to the higher purposes of agents, clubs and sponsors.

For the lover of football it is one of those moments that will stay in the memory forever. A goal that is only comparable to George Weah's in the AC Milan–Verona game. Or to Maradona's second goal against England in 1986. Three actions that refuse to submit to existing logic and knowledge of the possibilities of foot and ball.

Even after ten slow-motion replays it's hard to understand exactly what happens.

When Ronaldo receives the ball, he has yet to free himself from the ruck of players. One is hanging onto his shirt, but it is already too late: the Brazilian escapes, beats five men, some of them twice. He twists his torso from left to right, opens trap-doors, threatens with feints, steps in, steps out. Opponents kick or grab (one tries to stop him with both arms) but they fall off him like drops of sweat.

The finish is of an improbable precision. Apparently off balance, with two men around him and the keeper right in front of him, he nets it flawlessly.

That one rush (which lasted fourteen seconds, the same time as Weah's) reflects everything that makes Ronaldo special. When he is taken in a body-check, he doesn't drop melodramatically, but simply bumps back. Ronaldo can break the worst breaker. Like a pinball he shoots through the enemy lines. A Brazilian with the granite physique of a German.

To guide the flood of invitations and interview requests into suitable paths, Ronaldo, on the advice of his agents, takes on a lawyer.

The man goes to work rigorously. Every interview will have to be paid for. *France Football*, the magazine that organises the vote for the world's best player (Ronaldo!), is the first victim. The French are dumbfounded, and then furious. That same day the policy is dropped.

In other cases, however, Oriola stays firm. Only for $35,000 will Ronaldo add lustre to a restaurant opening. However, he is no marionette. When Cindy Crawford comes to Barcelona to launch a new Omega watch, the Brazilian is among the invitees. On the spot he is offered large sums to pose with Crawford for the cameras. Ronaldo refuses. 'They should have asked Cindy Crawford to pose with *me*,' he says afterwards.

11. *The happiness of the* Seleção

When Ronaldo arrives in Paris during the Tournoi de France, by TGV from Lyon, he finally has time to talk. The circles under his eyes and his somewhat swollen face suggest that he is at the end of his tether. 'I am tired,' he agrees.

The risk of an early burn-out seems real, but Ronaldo says: 'I am only twenty years old. I can take more than a player of thirty. Also, I am used to playing a lot. As a child I played football all day.'

He has developed an entirely new vision of his possible move to Inter. 'I don't care where I play next year. Inter or Barcelona – the Brazilian team remains the most important thing for me.'

What makes Brazil so special?

'Everything. The atmosphere, the happiness. The *Seleção* is the only team where I am never criticised for my so-called egotism. Nobody ever complains that he is being passed over. You'll never see one Brazilian chastise another the way Frank and Ronald de Boer do it, with those horrible gestures.'

Alexandre Martins and Reinaldo Pitta, Ronaldo's agents, represent a type of businesspeople who are the same the world over. Young bright men. Jeans, informal approach. Diplomatic in their choice of words, lean on the telephone. Types who can step seamlessly from one type of business to another. Ronaldo could have had worse luck. They make a very capable impression. I would entrust them with my financial fate immediately.

Martins pours a glass of water. He would rather have a beer, but his body won't allow it. He's still taking penicillin for a cold and a sore throat, the product of many flights to football clubs.

It's half past two in the morning, a few hours after Brazil have beaten England 1–0. 'Terrible game,' says Martins, who saw just one special moment: when Shearer and Ronaldo kicked each other. 'Before the match I told Ronaldo, "You should shake

Shearer's hand." Always a nice picture: Ronaldo and Shearer, the most expensive footballers in the world. Instead of being grateful, Shearer kicks Ronaldo in the balls. Did you see how upset Ronaldo looked? But he gave him one back.'

12. Footballer of the Year

Bobby Charlton's taxi is arriving. A brown squirrel opens the door and helps him get out. After Charlton comes Pelé, who is guided to the entrance of the Convention Centre by Mickey Mouse. Franz Beckenbauer is greeted by Donald Duck, while Rinus Michels has to make do with Goofy's helping hand.

FIFA used to show its face only when there was a championship to organise. But now it too is in the grip of promotion and marketing. With an eye on the World Cup in France, FIFA is staging the vote for the world's best player of the year in Eurodisney, Paris. That is to be the site of the International Football Hall of Champions. Franz Beckenbauer, Bobby Charlton, Stanley Matthews, Pelé, Johan Cruijff, Alfredo di Stefano, Lev Yashin, Ferenc Puskas, Michel Platini, Eusebio and Rinus Michels are the first *all-time favourites* to be honoured with a place in this museum.

Except for Matthews, Di Stefano, Cruijff and Yashin (who is dead) all the heroes are present at Eurodisney. FIFA has even put them in a forum, so that the press can sup from their knowledge once again.

They don't have much to say. Bobby Charlton and Beckenbauer tease each other about the World Cup final of 1966. Pelé mumbles something about the educational value of football, and speaks his veto over the admission of Maradona into the Hall of Fame, because the latter, given his white-powdered life, is hardly an example to youth. Rinus Michels explains once again what exactly 'total football' is.

They are also asked which of the quartet of nominated players (Ronaldo, Dennis Bergkamp, Roberto Carlos and Zinedine Zidane) they would choose as World Player of the Year. Ronaldo of course! Who could keep that title from the winner of the Golden Shoe (for the best shooter in Europe), the winner of the Golden Ball (for European Player of the Year) and the best footballer in Brazil (chosen by his colleagues)?

Only Rinus Michels has a reservation. 'If you only look at spectacle and goals, then Ronaldo is the best,' says the old master in creaky English. 'But if you judge it as coach and professional, then the team deserves the most attention. In that case I choose Zidane.'

That evening, in front of an audience of journalists, football directors and agents with mobile phones – a strange ratatouille of dinner jackets, wild ties and overbrowned faces – the official result is announced. Michels turns out to have been a lone voice. The 120 national team managers who make up the electorate vote overwhelmingly for spectacle and goals, and thus for Ronaldo.

The Brazilian receives the trophy from the hands of Pelé, and is as laconic as ever. 'It's not nothing to become the first player to be voted Player of the Year twice. I thank all my trainers and coaches.' Like a Sun King he accepts the congratulations of the assembled celebrities. Some – including Bobby Charlton – are completely unknown to him.

'Will you get a picture of him with my husband?' Mrs Michels implores one of the photographers.

Winning the league for Inter Milan and scoring more than thirty goals – that was the challenge Ronaldo set himself when he began this season in Serie A. He started fluently. After eight matches he had scored six goals, almost his normal average.

Then the production slowed and the wonderchild discovered what everyone had foretold: Italy is no Holland or Spain.

'Italy is still the land of *catenaccio*, even if they don't use the word anymore,' he said after the award ceremony in the Disney centre. 'Now they talk about *ben messo* (well arranged) but it comes down to the same thing. Every team plays from defence. They let the opponent come, and then they surround you, cement you in and crush you to death. Every match I have three, four defenders with me. Thanks to my speed I can sometimes break away. But usually the first man brings me down.'

He denies the rumours that he is discontented in Italy. 'I feel in my place with Inter, and I think I can play there for years. We have a team with strong internal ties. And I'm not afraid of a little resistance. A top-class player can only get better in Italy. Because the bit parts are also well performed, you automatically play a speed higher, with more concentration.'

Moreover, Italy is the land of limitless adoration. Players are turned into saints, mythological heroes, and that offers great advantages. It allows him to dole out the golden elixir of his talent with a little more measure. 'In Holland you have to show a trick ten times to get people clapping. In Italy they're satisfied with just one move.'

Last year Ronaldo played seventy-three matches. If he isn't playing for Inter, he is flying around the world to appear for Brazil in demonstration matches organised by Nike, sponsor of both Brazil and Ronaldo. The rest of his days he spends in airports and hotels, in press rooms and TV studios. A claustrophobic life. Outside a small circle of family, agents, team-mates, coaches and club directors he doesn't see anybody. But Ronaldo doesn't complain. 'If even I have something to complain about, then who doesn't?'

His blitheness contrasts sharply with reports that appeared

in the Italian press at the end of 1997. *La Gazetta dello Sport* said Ronaldo had fallen into depression during the Confederations Cup in Riyadh. After reading a newspaper which forecast a Maradona-like descent for him unless he quickly reduced his overload, he burst into tears in front of his room-mate Cesar Sampaio.

Zagalo, Brazil's coach, protected Ronaldo and left him out for a couple of matches. Zagalo had another explanation for Ronaldo's collapse. His star was suffering from the burden of having to lead Brazil to its fifth world championship. 'Leave Ronaldo alone,' he begged the Brazilian press. 'The boy has it hard enough. No other footballer has ever gone the way he is going.'

Shortly before leaving for Riyadh, Ronaldo returned to PSV for a couple of days. He treated his former team-mates to the farewell for which there had been no time when he left in 1996. First they went go-carting, and then clubbing in Belgium. The next day he visited PSV's training ground to see Dick Advocaat. 'Now that you're here, you might as well train with us,' said the PSV coach, and Ronaldo did. On borrowed shoes. 'That characterises the boy,' says Advocaat later, still enjoying the moment.

Advocaat didn't spot anything like unwillingness or an approaching burn-out. 'He seemed to me the same as always. Cheerful, happy. Some people say he's childish, but I think he's very mature and intelligent. Ronaldo knows exactly what he has to do and what he doesn't.'

Ronaldo doesn't intend simply to win his team another World Cup. Ronaldo, as ever, is aiming for personal success. He plans to break the record of Just Fontaine, who scored thirteen goals in one World Cup.

Last year Nike built Brazil a new headquarters. The conference rooms are called '1958', '1962', '1970' and '1994', after the years in which Brazil won the World Cup. One conference room has no name. The plan is to call it '1998'.

'But if Brazil wins the World Cup and I score more than thirteen goals, then they can name the room after me,' says Ronaldo, a heavenly anachronism in an age when football is bunged up with tactical tasks, all players have to be able to defend, and freebooting forwards who can bewitch little boys of all countries are as scarce as death's head moths in the centre of London.

Parts of this story first appeared in Hard Gras, *the Dutch literary football magazine. Translated by Simon Kuper.*

brasil

LUIS FERNANDO VERISSIMO

I Blame it on Black Beans

A spectre haunted the Brazilian team in California: the lack of material. Our worst adversary before the first match, against Russia, in the 1994 World Cup, was the lack of material. The Brazilian delegation was surrounded by a formidable journalistic and advertising apparatus that needed subjects in order to function. An enormous grinder of new facts which, with the lack of material, would end up devouring its own teeth. Or, making up catastrophes if only to break the routine. Now, the team itself wanted routine. The manager, Parreira, must have considered routine a calming bath, a warm lake of tranquillity in which to settle, safe from new developments, until the first game. All controversies had been settled or, if they hadn't been settled, there were no other viable alternatives, which adds up to being the same. The players were the same as usual. He already knew how the team should play and wasn't about to change his convictions. All the team had to do was to train, train some more, and take care not to sprain an ankle. The last thing Parreira wanted, in his routine bathtub, was for someone to run in crying, 'Romário eloped with the chambermaid!' However, the press and the sponsors needed, urgently, for Romário to elope with the chambermaid.

I was surprised that more theses had not popped up about the firing of the lady in charge of the nutrition, who didn't want the team to have the famous Brazilian black bean stew with their meals. It had been a promising subject which the media machine tasted and spat out in contempt. A defensible thesis had been that Parreira himself had vetoed the nutritionist.

'But, Parreira, she is right. Black bean stew is not food for athletes.'

'Can't you see? I want the black beans . . .'

'Why, Parreira?'

'To share the guilt! If we win the Cup, the glory belongs to everyone. Should we lose, the guilt will be all mine. I need alibis. I need accomplices. The black beans, the fat pork chops, the meat that goes with it . . .'

'But, Parreira . . .'

'I want to be able to declare, "It wasn't the strategy, it was the pork!" I'm not going to be banished alone.'

The fact was that Parreira was living his last days as a reasonably common citizen. Afterwards he'd either be a saint or a condemned man.

II World Cups

In Mexico, in 1986, the Brazilian press forces were decimated by the runs. We had had nothing to do with the genocidal conquest of Cortez, centuries before, but Montezuma's Revenge does not discriminate: it gives the runs to all foreigners. What Dante would have called the *cagotto*. The cautious had arrived with the firm disposition to avoid Mexican food, surviving on tea and crackers. It did no good: tea and crackers also gave them the runs. Nobody was immune, with the exception of some with asbestos-lined stomachs. There was nothing else one could do but to cry for mercy to the God of Colic. No alternative diet helped. Chicken broth, for instance, was extremely dangerous.

And the time zone conspired against our deadlines and our intestines. Stopping for lunch would have been impossible; one depended on breakfast to stay up all day long. The morning meal's options were displayed at a garish buffet, on tropical allegories, in the hotel's restaurant. Only those, who after a night of liquid insomnia are forced to choose between scrambled eggs with multicoloured peppers and various avocado pastes to break their fast, understand the true meaning of the expression 'bluarrrgh!'. On top of that, Zico and Sócrates wasted those penalty kicks!

In Torino, four years later, the challenge was, firstly, to find restaurants still open when we were through with the day's work and, secondly, not to grow overweight on Italian food. Indigestible was only our manager, Lazaroni. And after the pasta there were the puddings, served at some of the most charming *gelatterie* of the world. And the ice creams. Huge ice creams of fruits or nuts. I knew that Nietzsche had reached the depths of his madness in Torino. Knowing Torino, I could not figure how the philosopher had not been regenerated at the city's cafés. No one was better equipped to savour life in Torino than Nietzsche. With his cowcatcher moustache, he would have been able to taste the same ice cream twice!

In California, we were within reach of Montezuma's resentments, but the food options were greater – and San Francisco is one of the gastronomic capitals of the United States. The truth is that I am complaining literally on a full belly. I don't believe I've been able to convince anyone that journalism is a priesthood and that covering the World Cup is a sacrifice. It is such a major privilege that a minor diarrhoea at times is even welcome to remind us that, beyond the world of football, real life goes on.

III Shaving

Football managers understand the makers of shaving devices. Their problems are similar. Football, too, has been practically the same since it was invented. Only the details change. The manner of playing football may be completely different today than it was years ago, as the shape of today's shaving devices has nothing in common with those of the time when Mr Gillette invented his practical blade, but the fundamental conception remains unaltered, and unalterable. And, yet, every year the makers of shaving devices must present a new product. Every year, their marketing departments ask the research departments to reinvent the devices in order to have something to promote. Two blades, three blades, floating blades, convergent blades, divergent blades, musical blades – anything for last year's device to become obsolete and the newfangled to become irresistible. Likewise, every football manager, on taking over a new team, must bring with him the implicit suggestion that he is about to reinvent the game.

The reasons given for a change of manager are many. The dismissed manager had lost *ambiance*, had lost the confidence, had lost his head. But the true reason is the secret hope that the new manager will gather the players in the middle of the pitch, open his satchel and pull out of it – surprise! – a new game. An unheard-of kind of football. A football that no one else has, being therefore invincible. The miracle as yet has not materialised, but every football manager is the promise of a reinvented football. That is why they lead the life of holy men, wandering through the scenery, between temporary refuges, fully aware that time is short between being adored and being unmasked, between the flattery and the stoning. He is either a saviour or a charlatan. There is no middle-of-the-road option.

Nor the option of good sense. The new manager cannot tell the team and its supporters that football is a boring game of repetition and patience, often decided by the outside-left who was selected by chance. Likewise he cannot emphasise that football is played with the foot, an organ so inattentive and hard to control that it might as well have been the Government's. Nor can he remind one of the fact that the opponent will field, perversely, a team with the same number of players who also want the ball, simply to confound us. It would be somewhat similar to a maker of shaving devices launching an expensive publicity campaign to announce there is nothing new. To say there is nothing more to be done, that the shaving devices have attained the full limitations of their possibilities of change, that this year's will be sensationally identical to last year's. 'And do look forward to next year's, still more similar!' Unthinkable. The manager must feed the illusion that the formula does exist and that a magical transformation is possible. And football needs this illusion.

Parreira, the Brazilian team's manager in 1994, was a charlatan, inasmuch as every football manager, as long as he is not able to pull a new game out of a satchel, is a *farceur*. But he might have presented something new at the World Cup in the United States. Four blades, for instance.

Translated by Chuck Woodward.

game boys

SIMON INGLIS

Sarah telephones, knackered, as always. In our house there is calm. I put aside my newspaper and listen. In her house, Matthew and his younger brother sound as if they're trying to inflict pain upon the wooden floorboards in their kitchen.

Above the clatter Sarah says, in passing, 'Oh, I didn't tell you, Matt's been picked for the school team on Saturday.'

'Fantastic,' I say. 'That'll be a real boost for his confidence.'

I'm thinking that Stephen would have been proud and that I really should make the effort. Checking my diary as we speak, I note that Villa are not playing on Saturday.

'You know, I'd love to see him play.'

In our bed-time stories Matt always scores the winning goal.

'Are you sure?' says Sarah. 'He'd be really pleased.' But remembering my own self-consciousness as a schoolboy player, I have my doubts. These are confirmed as Matt picks up the telephone and insists absolutely that I do not come to watch him.

A forced laugh conceals my awkwardness. How well does a ten-year-old know his own mind? Am I being rejected or does he simply have stage fright?

I can hardly tell. I am not his father. I am not anyone's father, and nor am I destined to be one. That's just the way the cards were dealt to me and my wife. Mostly it's not a problem, but somehow football – that bond which men share so effortlessly with boys – always manages to penetrate my defences.

'Please don't come,' Matt continues to insist in that plaintive voice he has perfected so well.

So I put on an old overcoat, cover my face with a scarf, pull a woolly hat low over my brow, and time my anonymous arrival for mid-way during the first half. Matt's team, I'm told by one of many waxed cotton-clad parents lining the touchline, are drawing 2–2.

A light drizzle has settled across north London. I smell the sweet slither of wet grass and the scents of assorted mothers under corporate brollies. No one there knows me. I could be the parent of one of the visiting team. I could be a lonely man with nothing else to do on a Saturday afternoon. Covered up as I am, I could be a pervert.

To make matters worse, I do not know how to behave.

My boy games were in provincial, state-school suburbia, over three decades ago. But this is fee-paying Finchley. On the pitch, both teams wear monochrome rugby-style shirts in sensible cotton and say 'sorry' to their opponents when they make rash tackles. They have names like Sebastian, William and Jeremy. The referee, one of Matt's teachers, has tousled hair and a poet's expression, haunted yet concerned. His rumpled track-suit, seemingly extracted from Billy Wright's kitbag, displays no polyester sheen, no flashes or logos. Only the boys' contoured boots and the goalkeepers' dayglo gloves are suggestive of the brand-led nineties. Otherwise, a timeless, comfortable ease pre-vails. If a teacher were to order me to change – 'Now Inglis!' – and enter the fray, I wouldn't hesitate or even wonder where the intervening years had gone. That seductive soft turf, those insistent white lines. This open expanse! Dammit. Game boys never grow up, they just grow.

Matt has not yet seen me, and nor will he, I resolve, until after the final whistle. He is, in any case, playing quite well, so why spoil things by confusing my own agenda with his.

So I hang back, affect circumspection, and try hard to figure out the rules for watching schoolboy matches. What comes first, the boys or the game? The boy, the one you've come to support, or his team? Is this how scouts feel when they come to check out a particular talent? Blinkered, focused, and perhaps even a touch proprietorial towards their quarry?

I opt for the blinkers, and suffer accordingly.

While the other spectators maintain a steady banter, exchanging convoluted tales of weekend cottage disasters with gripes about nannies or flute teachers, I fight the urge to berate Sebastian for fluffing a pass that would have put Matt clear on goal. I keep shtum when Sam selfishly tries to dribble through the other school's defence, even though Matt hovers unmarked on the wings. I've seen the documentaries – the ugliness of frothing parents, cranking up their offspring's aggression from the touchlines. But then, I'm not a parent.

At home, in these boys' natural milieux – for theirs are unquestionably homes in which the word milieu is entirely natural – I presume that the rules of association require all boys to share and share alike, to control their anger, to suffer the slings and arrows of outrageous fortune and not to take arms against their younger siblings. Never mind Tom and Jerry. Take a lesson from *Toy Story*. And then we'll all talk about it.

'Does Matt ever talk to you about Stephen?' Sarah sometimes asks.

'No, he doesn't,' I have to confess. Matt and I do talk, all the time. He knows that Stephen and I used to play tennis together a lot. He knows that we went to football matches. But as for big stuff, I find myself in the John Wayne camp. Hey guys, I know what a couch is for.

Nevertheless, here I am with the other boys' parents on the playing fields of Finchley, being 'supportive' rather than a 'supporter'. Remembering that it's not the winning that counts, but the taking part.

Until an incongruously raucous voice suddenly pierces the grey afternoon.

'Huuuugo, get stuck in! Fight for it!'

And to my dismay I realise that the scarf has slipped and that the voice is my own. In the heat of the battle I have broken my vow of silence. Football has yet again got the better of me.

Matt spots me instantaneously, neither glares (thank goodness) nor smiles (oh well), and then, having flicked his ginger mop as if he were David Beckham stung by the orders of Glenn Hoddle, chases a lost cause with a sudden burst of commitment. Already he is familiar with the postures a professional player will adopt when he realises that the cameras are upon him. I like that in a kid, and from then on, shout without inhibition.

As we gather for tea and biscuits in the pavilion afterwards, one of the boys asks me rather gravely, 'Are you Matt's father?'

'No he's not,' Matt interjects firmly. 'He's my godfather.'

We've had to confront this situation several times before, so I don't blame Matt for his insistence, even though occasionally it makes me feel like an interloper. But what else is he supposed to say? 'No, my father's dead.'

Besides which, all the other parents have turned up in Range Rovers or People Movers. I came on the Number 13 bus.

As the lumps on Stephen's body grew even larger and deadlier, he asked me to look out for Matt, to be more than a godfather. I promised, but quaked inwardly. As big stuff goes, this was immense. A dying friend, solemn oaths, a baffled three-year-old Matt in the next room.

Psychologists reckon that the first three years are the most important in forging the father–son relationship. If true, that's all Matt was destined to get. Not only that, but Stephen patently never got round to talking football with his son.

Hence the stuff got bigger. In the final week Stephen made another request. He beseeched me not to allow his wife's family and their traditional allegiance to sway Matt in his future choice of club. Grandpa Sol, various uncles and cousins on her side were all Gooners. Stephen was not. His entreaty had little to do with football, nor even with any particular animus he might have felt for Arsenal. What mattered was the legacy. For a small but significant part of Stephen to live on forever in his son's psyche.

Not a lot to ask when your life is ebbing away at the age of thirty-four. But a lot to ask of a son when the team you support happens to be Tottenham.

In *Oliver Twist*, Mr Grimwig says that he knows of only two sorts of boys. 'Mealy boys and beef-faced boys.' My rather more limited experience suggests that there is only one type of boy. The boy that says 'I know'.

'Matt, see that? That's what they call a bicycle kick.'

'I know.'

'Hey, Matt, looks like pressure is building up on the pound again.'

'I know.'

Little boys cannot bear to admit that there are some things they just don't know. Believe me, I know.

I also know from experience with other young debutants that taking a boy to his first ever game, a boy who is not your son and whose parents are not especially bothered about football, is both an immense privilege and an awesome obligation.

'For heaven's sake, if anyone knows the ropes it should be Simon. Of course he'll be safe, isn't that right Simon?'

'Absolutely, no problem. I won't leave his side. He'll have a great time.'

I feel like the Victorian uncle given leave to introduce a young buck to the pleasures of the night. Better someone steers the lad in the direction of a decent bordello than let him fend for himself on the street, what?

But what if I get it wrong?

To be child-less, but not child-free, is to tread a fine line. Nephews, nieces, teenage neighbours and Tamagotchi-clutching weekend guests the Inglis household will happily welcome, if only on short-term loan. But having few responsibilities of our own has made my wife and I perilously prey to irresponsibility. It takes only one misplaced word or an unwittingly incorrect act to have parents hauling us into the naughty corner for a reminder of what is and what is not 'appropriate behaviour'. Shit. We non-parents have to be so careful.

And what if the boy is not so game and ends up hating every minute of his first match? Will that be it, for life? My fault. How could I be so crass and uncaring? How was I supposed to know that little Johnny had developed a phobia about turnstiles ever since he was turned away from the Pepsi Max Big One in Blackpool for being 'too small'?

Then there is the question of how much one interprets the action or simply allows the event to wash over the child, like a wave of mystery. Plus of course, what if he asks you to explain the offside rule? I mean, I know it, but well . . . you know.

And what if he loves every minute? What if the game boy becomes besotted? Sticking up posters on his bedroom wall is one thing, but the hard stuff will follow soon enough, you mark my words. Replica shirts, scarves, duvet covers, lampshades, satellite dishes. Not to mention the cost of match tickets.

So I don't mention the cost of the match tickets, or the likely accumulation of costs over the next, say, fifty years of entrapment. I'm not his dad, after all. I can stand in the club shop and say, quite convincingly, 'No, no, no!' till Matt gets quite bored.

Or if pushed I can add, 'Well, let's see what your mum says when we get home.'

Besides which, much, much easier, by far, is to invest in sweets.

I learnt this first from my nephew, aged six, at Edgeley Park, where he consumed a four-ounce bag of bon-bons, a Twix, a can of Coke and a liquorice swirl, and that was just before half-time. Several years later and he's got all the usual teenage spots. But he is saving up for a season ticket.

To ease Matt's first big match outing, therefore, I allowed him to wolf his way through a tube of Rolos, half of my pear drops, and most impressively of all, an entire bag of wine gums in the time it took me to expostulate, 'Don't you think you should leave some for the second half?'

But then he also said at half-time, 'This is brilliant, Simon. Thanks ever so much for bringing me.' And I would have hugged him there and then except for the fact that he would have died of embarrassment, or worse, have crushed the Mars Bar I'd kept tucked away in my inside coat pocket for emergencies.

'Matt, you do realise that we're going to have supper when we get home.'

'I know.'

'Which means that we'll just share the one bag of chips between us after the game, all right?'

'Cool.'

No doubt the adults would mark me down for inappropriate behaviour, peddling sugar and grease to innocents at the school gates. But I reckon that small game boys need all the solace they can get during their debuts.

Oh sure, they've seen games on the telly and think they can imagine exactly what it'll be like.

'Now we must be very careful, there's going to be a huge crowd today.'

'I know.'

But they don't. Frisky little smart-arses who parade their independence in the playground or run free and easy in the park always, always, always grasp anxiously for a big boy's hand in a football crowd. I offer mine, it is accepted, and as flesh meets flesh a current leaps from his trusting little hand to mine, rippling through my system until a message somewhere in my brain lights up. The message reads: 'Hold tight, but not too tight.' Then it says, 'This is what it's like to be a dad.' And then finally it adds: 'Nice, isn't it?'

Perplexed but momentarily proud also, I see people step aside thoughtfully. I hear the kindly words of turnstile operators and older fans, reassuring, cajoling, welcoming the novice to this man's world. I see other small boys around and want to ruffle their hair and say, 'Hello little 'un, welcome to our world.'

A noisy world it is too, up in the stands. Noisier than they had ever imagined.

In the beginning Matt was frightened. 'Why is everyone shouting?' he pleaded, covering his ears. He hated it when the home team scored. He'd never heard such a deafening roar.

Well he wouldn't, would he. There is nothing in any primary school classroom or at any children's party, however unruly, that can quite prepare a child for the sound of ten, twenty or thirty thousand humans erupting into communal pandemonium. Nor, I find, does *Match of the Day* necessarily attune a child's ears to the subtle variations of a football crowd's utterances.

'Was that a goal?'

'No, not that time.'

'So why's everyone shouting?'

'It went into the side netting.'

'So why doesn't that man behind us shut up?'

'He thinks the players can hear him.'

'But they can't, and anyway he's horrible. Can't you tell him to shut up?'

'No I can't. Here, have some Mars Bar.'

'Oh cool.'

Worst of all are the toilets. Pressed up against nylon car-coats and sweaty polyester in the shuffling queues, once through the doors the diminutive first-timer finds himself catapulted into a free-for-all of flailing elbows and Brobdingnagian backsides. Somewhere up ahead, now becoming closer and closer with each push, shove and fought-over gap, cascading urinals loom large at face height. Left and right, hairy appendages spout steaming piss. The boy backs away from the splashing trough, his urge suddenly lost in paralysed terror. Do you coax or withdraw? Do you go first to offer reassurance? Suddenly you are a stranger to him. This is all too intimate. You are not his dad.

In all the recent books about boys and boys' troubles it is men who seem to take the rap. Poor loves. Always looking for an escape, we are. Always seeking to avoid the housework and the childcare. Immersing ourselves in nonsense; tactics, transfer news, league tables, statistics.

'Great! You can't remember your old aunty's birthday but you can remember who won the FA Cup in 1976.'

An American writer, Mariah Burton Nelson, reckons that the stronger women get, the more men love football. It's a nice line, but I prefer to imagine that the stronger women get the more *they* love football too. Even if they don't want it for themselves, they can surely see how useful it is to us. Our space. Their space. Mars and Venus. Mars and Twix. Gullit and Rix. Southampton. Beat Man U one-nil. In 1976 I mean. Everyone knows that. Ask me another.

Another feminist writer has claimed that the very notion of 'fatherhood' has been evolved by men only recently, purely to gratify our innate sense of self-importance, whereas in primitive societies women managed perfectly well on their own, feeding and clothing their children and needing us blokes only for defensive duties. So that's all right then. Come on boys, we can go to the match after all.

But most experts also seem to agree that for modern-day boys, the truly exciting thing about fathers is that they carry with them the mysteries of the outside world. While mums represent familiarity, home and succour, all of which occupy most of our earliest years, dads get to pick up the ball and run out of the house. Dads' world smells different.

My dad's world had some wonderful smells. The oil of cloves in his dental surgery, the leather upholstery of his Singer Gazelle, the mown grass of the lawn and, best of all, the intoxicating great outdoors, clinging to his clothes after a round of golf. But he never took me to football. That much I owe to my older brother Jonathan. He was my guide at Villa Park, when I was seven and he was eleven. Then he became a father himself. And now, like Stephen, Jonathan is dead too, and I wonder if one day his little boy will ever reach out for my hand at a football match and take that journey into a different world.

And if he doesn't show an interest? Or if he does, but the hand he reaches out for belongs to another, how will I react? Will I sulk and tell myself, 'It should have been me'?

As it happened, I made no promises to Jonathan, about his son, about his daughter, about his wife, about football or anything. Unlike with Stephen there was simply no time, no warning. Here one minute, gone the next. Brother gone. Best friend gone.

But then no one ever promised me a rose garden.

So there we are, two survivors, Matt and I, sitting in the North Bank Stand at Highbury, glad we didn't take Sarah's advice and wear long-johns. Glad we didn't bring the carrier-bag full of supplies that she'd prepared. Come on, mum, we're big boys now. We're off to Arsenal, not the Arctic.

Matt is in good form. So good, in fact, that he's singing.

'*We're the North Bank, the North Bank, the North Bank High-bu-reee!*'

As are the two lads sitting behind us, lungs the size of prize marrows, brains the size of peas. Does Matt know what a wanker really is? Or a shirt-lifter? Should I turn around and ask them to tone down their language? I'd like to, but they're by no means alone, and in any case Matt's own attempts to match them are so touchingly innocent by comparison. He squeals 'Chicken!' as a Blackburn defender passes back to the goalkeeper.

'Great keeper, Tim Flowers,' I say, in the cause of fair play.

'I know,' says Matt. 'He'd be England's number one if it wasn't for Seaman.'

Later in the game, with Arsenal now losing, the Clock End starts a chant. Both lads behind us join in, and before I can make out the words, Matt is on his feet too, singing with relish.

'*Stand up, if you hate Tottenham! Stand up, if you hate Tottenham . . .*'

I want to sit him down and tell him what is in my heart; about my final promise to Stephen, about his wishes for Matt's future, and how much I miss my afternoons with Stephen at White Hart Lane and with Jonathan at Villa Park.

But I say nothing because his team are 3–1 down at home and anyway, aren't things tough enough for him as it is?

every fan's dream

SIMON VEKSNER

'So, Carl Young, like many other multi-millionaires, you've recently bought a Premiership football club. Why?'

'Hello John,' said Carl Young, adjusting his microphone. 'Well, I've been a City fan for over twenty-five years, so it's actually a dream I've had for some time.'

'But don't most fans dream of *playing* for their team?' asked the interviewer.

'Ha ha ha,' laughed the mild-mannered software magnate.

'Joking aside,' the interviewer said, 'if I can just turn to the manager for a moment, Ron Jangles. Two weeks after the announcement, and you've already spent £12 million of your new chairman's money. Tell us about that.'

'Yes, John. I've brought in Gerry Snelling, whom I expect to score a lot of goals for the club. Then I've also brought in Hardmandze. He's the captain of the Georgian national side, very experienced lad, and he should just tighten things up at the back for us.'

'£12 million in two weeks – that's a lot of money to spend.'

'Well, that's my job – to spend the chairman's money in whatever way I think will win us trophies. We finished seventh last year, which isn't *bad*, but a club this size should be finishing a bit higher than that, or possibly winning a cup. I've been fortunate enough to win the league before —'

'Yes, I know – and best of luck this season, Ron.'

'Thanks. Yes, having won it as a *player*, I —'

'*Thank you*, Ron Jangles. City manager Ron Jangles there, along with chairman Carl Young—'

'—*my goal now*,' continued Jangles, 'is to do it as a manager.'

After leaving the Radio 5 Live studios (excited, because he had met Alan Green), Carl Young made his way to the Archetype PLC headquarters building.

'Hi Carl!'

'Hi Carl!'

'Hi Carl – I've got a great new idea for the 4-series Transducer...'

Carl's employees had poor skin and wore Hi-Tec trainers, but they were passionate about computers. And Archetype was a happy ship because no one had ever been made redundant. Carl met his employees in person once a month to listen to their ideas, and the company had recently beaten Microsoft in the world *Doom* championships.

Finally, Young reached his office, and sat down in his leather-backed swivel-chair. He began sheafing through the neat stack of papers that awaited his attention, but he found his eyes irresistibly drawn to the perspex display-case that stood by the window. This display-case housed the first computer Young had ever owned, a Sinclair ZX Spectrum (16K version).

When he was very young, the other boys wouldn't let him play football in the playground with them, because he had a Rubik's cube. Later, it was because he wore glasses and liked computers. If you were good at Maths, you weren't allowed to like football, but Young loved football and played secretly in his living room with a mangy old Dunlop Fort tennis ball, imagining he was seventies City striker Rodney Sideburn.

'Not long now,' said Young to himself.

At 9.30 a.m. next morning, Carl Young steered his dark

green Volvo into the players' car park which, curiously, was empty. Hoisting his kit bag onto his shoulder, the City chairman gingerly made his way towards the dressing room, dressed casually in business shirt and a brand new pair of Marks & Spencer's jeans.

'Mr Young!' exclaimed a surprised Ron Jangles, and he and his Number Two Terry McDoormat stood up so suddenly that McDoormat spilled his tea (white with three sugars) over his *Racing Post*.

'Please, call me Carl,' said Young. 'Er, where are the players? I thought training started at ten?'

McDoormat looked puzzled.

'Oh they're on their way, don't you worry, Mr Young,' said Jangles, putting an arm over his chairman's shoulder, where his hand came to rest on the kit bag.

'Oh,' said Young, putting the bag down on the floor, 'I'm a keen jogger, and I thought I might join in with training, if that's OK.'

McDoormat's mug became suspended in mid-air, *en route* to his mouth, which remained open.

Ron Jangles looked into Young's eyes. He saw two problems: 1) Young was crazy. 2) He was the chairman.

'Of course it's OK, Mr Young,' said Jangles. 'Terry—'

'Yes, gaffer?'

'Find some kit for Mr Young.'

'Yes, gaffer.'

'There's no need,' said Young. 'I have the full strip right here.'

He pulled his City top out of his kit bag and showed it proudly to the two men. No one had thought to send him any kit after he'd bought City, but that didn't matter, because Young had already bought both kits, home and away, as he did every season, from the club shop. He even had the socks.

'We don't train in the strip, Mr Young. Terry'll get you some training kit.'

McDoormat scuttled off and returned a short while later with a training top marked '37'.

'Can't I wear No. 9?' asked Young.

'That's Gerry Snelling's number,' started McDoormat, then, seeing the glare in his manager's eyes, added: 'Er, No. 9, of course,' and set off back down the corridor.

By 10.15 some of the players had started to arrive, and as they hung up their Versace suits and bantered with each other, completely ignoring the presence of their chairman, Young eavesdropped frantically for a conversation-entering opportunity.

'I'll tell you who'll be the biggest danger tomorrow night,' opined City goalie Mike Fitzsimmons, who, in terms of ability, was possibly the best goalkeeper in the Premier League.

Tomorrow night . . . the friendly against Bayern Lederhosen . . . Bayern had a prolific striker . . . what was his name? . . . Horst something?

'Renton Boy,' continued Fitzsimmons. 'He's got six pounds on Hoplite, and Mentor beat him by a neck on the all-weather.'

Young began studying the dressing-room floor, which was scored with thousands and thousands of stud-marks.

Hardmandze the Georgian arrived, a somewhat incongruous figure with his stone-wash jeans and seventies hairstyle. Suddenly, Young felt a wave of sympathy for the big defender, thousands of miles from home, unable to speak a word of English . . . Young desperately wanted to say something to him . . . and yet, and yet . . . what could *he* possibly have to say that would be of interest to the captain of the Georgian national team?

'Did you really train with the players?' asked Kathy a week later, as they drove to Ron Jangles' pre-season barbecue.

'Yes I did,' said Young.

'And did you wear your glasses?'

'Er, yes,' said Young (this was a private joke between the couple – minus glasses, Young had run into a tree when they went jogging together on their first date at Stanford Business School) 'and guess who came first in the two-mile run?'

'No way!'

'Yes,' said Young, inwardly wishing he felt prouder of his achievement – for the City squad was drastically unfit. Wide-midfielder Andy Darrington had pulled up after fifty yards, moaning: 'It's my Achilles ... or cruciate. Maybe.' And club captain Tony Sayers had stopped to throw up in a rose-bush. It had been, explained Sayers, a 'heavy night'.

'This must be it, honey,' said Kathy, as the wrought-iron gates of 'RonFork' swung into view.

Young parked up behind Gerry Snelling's Porsche.

'Welcome, welcome to my humble abode,' said Ron Jangles, coming out to meet them, an attractive blonde woman in tow. 'Mrs Young, a pleasure. I understand you're American?'

'That's right.'

'My wife's foreign too – she's from Glasgow, ha ha ha ha.'

'Ha ha ha,' said Mrs Jangles.

Jangles' guests were standing in two groups: City's black players and their wives at one end of the garden, the rest of the squad and their wives at the other.

Terry McDoormat presented the Youngs with two plates of food.

'Oh, I'm sorry, I should have said,' said Kathy. 'Carl and I are vegetarians.'

McDoormat looked aghast. In a long career, which had begun at Bury and taken in Everton, Leeds and Leicester, with a spell at Roma and two England caps along the way, he thought he had seen it all.

Mrs Jangles hand-cooked a Safeways cheese-and-tomato pizza for the Youngs, while Carl watched fascinated as the players' seven-year-old sons, all scaled-down versions of their fathers with long brown limbs and pudding-bowl haircuts, discussed the latest transfer news while tearing through a mountain of primary-coloured foods.

Later, the footballers went into the living room to have a game of PlayStation, while their sons played football in the garden.

Young spotted his wife – not hard, as she was the only dark-haired woman at the gathering – sitting alone by the ornamental pond.

'Come on, team,' he said, crouching down in front of her. 'Let's go, shall we?'

Young had never heard 25,000 people say 'What?' at the same time. Ron Jangles hadn't said 'What?' when Young had told him – he hadn't seemed surprised at all, which he wasn't, because he'd already predicted it and had simply dealt with the news by sessioning whisky with McDoormat in the players' bar, where they'd reached the conclusion that their chairman was a bloody fool.

When the PA announced that City's new chairman would be starting the first match of the season not in the directors' box, but on the pitch, the 25,000 people in the ground all said 'What?' at the same time, except for John Motson, who said: 'Now that *is* a surprise. I'd be very interested to hear your view on that, Trevor.'

For Young, the first half passed in a blur of sheer embarrassment as, dripping with opposition saliva, his shins whacked blue through his shin-pads, Young mis-hit every pass he tried to make and was caught off-side four times (so humiliating – the ref stops the game and it's *all your fault*). Worst of all, the fans began groaning audibly every time he touched the ball. And as a result every time he touched the ball, he lost it.

At half-time (0–0), Ron Jangles took Young to one side.

'How are you feeling, Mr Young?' he asked in a low voice, so none of the players would hear.

'*I'm not coming off*,' snapped Young, in whom pain and humiliation had turned to bloody-mindedness. 'All I want is to score one goal. *One goal.* Is that too much to ask for twenty-five years of devotion and twelve million pounds? I'm going to stay up front and just goal-hang, OK? Er, tell the lads, please.'

Jangles rubbed his chin very slowly.

'Whatever you say, Mr Young,' he said.

In the second half, City played like kids playing football in the park with a dog – passing the ball to their eager mutt and watching amused as he dribbled it awkwardly for a few yards before losing control.

And yet, one opportunity *did* come.

City were awarded a corner. Snelling headed the ball back across the box, it fell to the opposition centre-forward but Hardmandze's groin-punch dispossessed him and the ball rolled across to Young. For one split second Young actually visualised the ball in the back of the net, before a dozen studs crunched into the top of his boot and the chance was gone.

Young limped around the pitch for a few more minutes but after once or twice receiving the ball and being unable to do more than dab limply at it with his agonised appendage, he signalled to be taken off.

He watched the rest of the game (there were three late goals – City winning 2–1) from the bench. And for the first time in his life Young was actually upset to see City win, because he had so much wanted to be a part of it.

Nevertheless, he decided he should go and congratulate the players.

There were loud roars coming from behind the dressing-room door. Young opened it. Immediately the City team, who were naked, ceased spraying each other with champagne and fell totally silent.

'Well done lads,' said Young, averting his eyes from Hardmandze's unfeasibly large penis.

There were a few mumbles of 'Thanks, Mr Young', and the odd cough. Young wondered whether he should spontaneously join in with their celebrations. But his presence seemed to be making them feel awkward.

'Carry on,' he said, and shut the door.

Miserable, Young made his way back down the corridor as renewed raucousness broke out behind him, and without knocking, he entered Ron Jangles' office where Jangles and McDoormat had their feet up on the desk, a bottle of whisky between them.

'Before you say anything Ron,' said Young, as the manager and his assistant scrambled to sit up, 'you were right.'

Jangles briefly caught his chairman's gaze but Young immediately looked away and said: 'You don't have to put me in the team any more.'

Jangles exhaled heavily.

'Mr Young, you're not a *bad* player,' he lied. 'I've seen plenty worse – we had worse at United when we won the league. Ha ha ha! But you're the *chairman*. With all due respect, Mr Young, your place is not in the team.'

'No,' agreed Young, suddenly looking up. 'Not in the starting line-up, anyway.'

Jangles and McDoormat did a double-take each.

'Not in the starting line-up . . .' stammered McDoormat.

'That's right – I want to be on the bench, and when we get a penalty, I'll come on and take it. We tend to get about four or five penalties a season so I should have a good chance of scoring.'

'But we've promised Gerry Snelling—' began McDoormat, but Jangles raised his hand, and Carl Young was duly named as a substitute and took his place on the bench, from where he cheered passionately for the team and courteously refrained from making tactical suggestions, until at long last, in the third match of the season, City were awarded a penalty.

Young strode confidently to the 'D', calmly placed the ball on the spot, and the opposing team's captain whispered in his ear: 'Mate, I hear your wife's been playing away.' This was a *blatant* attempt to put him off, and there was no way he was going to let it get to him. But what a ridiculous thing to say! It was quite impossible that Kathy, than whom no man could have a wife more loyal . . . this guy didn't even *know* Kathy, had never so much as laid eyes on her . . . the fact that he could even *suggest* such a thing was just *so* ridiculous it made him really quite *angry*.

And so Young blasted his penalty five feet over the bar.

He never told Kathy what the player had said to him.

'Give it up,' she said. 'You're great at what you do – you don't need to be a soccer star as well. No one can be good at everything. Don't embarrass yourself, honey.'

Young nodded. A lecture from your wife is different from a university lecture because you cannot ask questions at the end.

But soon Young became impatient for the chance to redeem himself, a chance which finally arrived half-way through the season, with City already 3–0 up in an away match against the league's bottom club. There could hardly have been a less pressurised time to come on and take a penalty. But the effect of 20,000 hostile fans singing: 'One Gerry Snelling, there's only one Gerry Snelling' was sufficient to make Young shoot weakly at the keeper.

That evening, in the players' bar, Ron Jangles drank five double whiskies and somehow found the resolve to confront his chairman.

'Your dream *can* become reality, Mr Young,' said Jangles expansively. 'But only through your money, not your footballing skills.'

'You're right,' said Young, who couldn't look Jangles in the eye because Jangles' head was swaying from side to side, so instead he looked out the window to the car-park, where he observed the Armani-clad Hardmandze showing a gaggle of City players his brand-new Mercedes SLK. 'My footballing skills are, let's be honest, inadequate.'

Jangles put down his whisky and, for the second time that season, put a hand over his chairman's shoulder.

'I've been a fool,' continued Young, as Jangles pawed at his back, like a camelhair-coated bear that had accidentally blundered into the players' bar, 'to think I could succeed without professional training.' Jangles' hand immediately ceased patting. 'I want Gerry Snelling to teach me how to take penalties.'

'Terry!'

'The key to a successful penalty,' said Gerry Snelling, placing the ball firmly on the penalty spot, 'is to get it in the back of the net.'

He strode nonchalantly up to the ball and whacked it past City's reserve-team keeper, who had been drafted in for the occasion because Mike Fitzsimmons, who in terms of ability was possibly the best goalkeeper in the Premier League, had begun to lose form due to stress caused by his gambling debts, and Jangles had unloaded him to Stockbridge Town for a cut-price £500,000.

'I see,' said Young, taking off his glasses and rubbing them on the front of his training top.

'It doesn't matter how you hit it, or which side of the keeper,' continued Snelling, placing a ball down for Young, 'the main thing is just to get it in.'

Young hit one, and scored.

'That's it!' encouraged Snelling. 'It's as simple as that.'

Young frowned.

'But what about the mental side?' he asked Snelling.

'The mental side?'

'Yes,' said Young, bouncing the ball on the ground, like a basketball. 'What do you *think about* when you take a penalty? Do you say to yourself: "My boot is a hammer", or anything like that?'

Snelling ran a hand through his mop of blond hair.

'No,' he said. 'I don't.'

Young cradled the ball against his narrow chest and sighed heavily.

'Wait a bit,' said Snelling, slowly. 'Sometimes I *do* say something to myself.'

'Yes?' urged Young.

'I say: "Gerry, you're the best!",' said Snelling. 'And I haven't missed a penalty yet. Except for in the Coca-Cola, which doesn't count.'

Later, Gerry Snelling invited Young to visit his beautiful home on the Herts/Essex border, where the two men spent a couple of hours getting drunk in the City forward's well-stocked bar/pool room.

'Nine goals. Nine sodding goals all season,' slurred Snelling, and launched the cue ball scudding off three cushions without hitting anything.

'But they were all good goals, Gerry —'

'There's sodding *mid*fielders have got more than that,' snarled Snelling, who had a pathological hatred for midfielders, because they never gave him enough quality ball, and he bent down once again over the table, though it occurred to Young that it should have been his shot now. Two shots, in fact. 'I'll be *out* at the end of the season. In the Southern Donkey League.'

'No, no, Gerry – Jangles likes you.'

Snelling was trying to focus on the cue ball but his face had suddenly reddened and his hand began shaking.

'Ron Jangles is a c***!' he shouted, and there was a great ripping sound as Snelling's cue tore into the cloth.

'Uh, I better be going—' began Young.

'Crystals!' enthused Snelling, dropping his cue on the table from where it bounced woodily to the floor. 'Less go down Crystals. You wanna be a professional footballer, you gotta go dahn the clubs.'

'Look, Gerry, I'm not sure . . .'

'Come on! It's Val's birfday, *all* the lads'll be there.'

'Val' was a nickname for Valentin Hardmandze, who had adapted extremely well to life in the Premiership. His command of English remained limited. However, he was dating a glamour model called Sabrina Pleasure and had written-off three Mercedes SLKs and two Jaguar XK8s.

'Come on, we've got to go now,' continued Snelling, tugging at the sleeve of Young's C&A ski jacket. Snelling paused. 'Except, I haven't shown you my bedroom yet.'

As he sat in Snelling's Porsche, wearing one of Snelling's black-and-grey broad-stripe Basi suits, chewing, like Snelling, on a stick of Orbit sugar-free gum, Carl Young suddenly realised what it is that separates the person of footballing ability from the professional footballer. It's not skill or fitness – there are thousands of fit and skilful players in pub sides up and down the country – the difference is one of lifestyle. Young could *buy* players. But he could never *be* one.

Next day, Kathy Young made her weekly call to her mother in Houston.

'Hi Mom . . . yeah, things are good . . . well, I'm kinda worried about Carl . . . yeah, he's under a lot of stress – you know, the stock price has been down recently, the City's worried that he's gone a little crazy with this soccer thing . . . no, actually he didn't go to work today, he's home sick – he went out with some of his soccer players last night, I think he must have eaten some bad food – there was puke in the downstairs bathroom this morning, or it could have been a bad reaction to some dental work he had done, he said something about never going in the dentist's chair again . . .'

That season, City finished only fourth in the Premiership. But they did win through to an FA Cup final against a young Stockbridge Town side that was capable of beating anyone on its day.

Young took up his usual place, next to Jangles and McDoormat on the bench.

'Good luck, Ron,' he said.

'Thank you, Mr Young.'

'You must be very proud of the lads.'

'Oh, tremendously. And we'll have a good crack at the league next year. That's my ambition now, to—'

'Just for once can't you shut up about the bloody league!' shouted McDoormat, moustache quivering, before adding quickly: 'Er, sorry, gaffer. Don't know what came over me there.'

McDoormat's temporary loss of servility was astonishing – but then, pressure does strange things to a man.

It was clearly affecting the players too, and the game remained 0–0 until the 90th minute, when Hardmandze came up for a corner and received an elbow in the face from the Stockbridge keeper, his former colleague Mike Fitzsimmons.

Penalty.

Young looked up into the stand towards where his wife was sitting. Her face was covered with both hands. And a scarf. Oh dear, even his own wife couldn't bear to watch. If he screwed this up, could he face her? Could he face himself? Could he live with the snide remarks that would undoubtedly appear in the Lex column of the *Financial Times*? And what about Gerry Snelling? Shouldn't he be giving his friend Gerry the chance to rescue his season?

As Young stood up from the bench, a great roar of joy arose from the Stockbridge fans, accompanied by a simultaneous and prolonged groaning from the City fans, and for a second, Young hesitated.

But only for a second. For what did it matter if Kathy, Ron Jangles, that grinning idiot Terry McDoormat, the software world, the City, the media, Gerry Snelling, the other players, the fans and indeed the entire country thought him a fool?

Wembley Stadium. The 90th minute of the FA Cup final. Scores level. And *you* coming on to take a penalty.

It had to be done.

Young ran onto the pitch and the Stockbridge fans burst into a deafening chorus of 'One Gerry Snelling'.

Ignore them . . . You've got to just block it out, Carl, that's what messed you up last time . . . put the ball down, turn around, five steps, turn around again . . . deep breath, visualise the ball going into the back of the net . . .

One Gerry Snelling
There's only one Gerry Snelling
One Gerry Snelling

. . . I'll hit it to the left . . . No, the right, the right . . . oh Christ, which way am I going to hit it? . . . there's 85,000 people in this ground, God knows how many millions watching on TV, I've made a big, big mistake . . . got to hit it now, got to hit it . . .

There's only one Gerry Snelling
One Gerry Snelling
One Gerry Snelling

. . . Carl, you're the best!

YYYYYYYYYY
EEEEEEEEEEE
HHHHHHHHHH
SSSSSSSSSSSS
!!!!!!!!!!!!!!!!!!!!!!!

Young's shot was tame, but Fitzsimmons had gone the wrong way. 1–0. Carl Young had won the FA Cup for City.

As he was mobbed by the players, Young did not even notice that his glasses had fallen off and been trampled into the Wembley turf.

Many days passed. City's victory entered the history books, the football season had been analysed, dissected and packaged into snappily edited highlights tapes, and the country had settled down to another summer of watery sunshine and England batting collapses.

But one night in late June, if anyone had happened to be at Scratchwood Services just off the M1, at two in the morning, they would have seen a late-model BMW creep quietly into the car-park and draw up near a red MGF.

Two men exited their cars, one of them carrying a canvas bag.

'Evening.'

'Evening.'

For three or four seconds, silence reigned.

'Now listen, if you so much as —'

'Oh, because, like, *you're* so *pure* . . .'

Angered, Ron Jangles launched the heavy hold-all high into the air, where it was expertly caught by the taller man. After all, in terms of ability, he was possibly the best goalkeeper in the Premier League.

remembering the nest

D.J. TAYLOR

Without wanting to embark on a wholesale anatomy of football supporting, allegiance to a particular line-up is usually of an a) territorial and b) generational nature. Thus should you be a Hungarian, say, born at any time before 1935, the chances are that your dream forward line would be Budai/Kocsis/Hidegkuti/ Puskas/Czibor. Anyone born in England after about 1950, on the other hand, would have to think very hard before discarding the Ball/Hunt/Hurst/Charlton (R.)/Peters option, even if, like Brian Glanville in his *The Story of the World Cup* (Faber £9.99), you could never understand why Hunt got the nod over dear old Jimmy Greaves. Steer the birth chronometer back to about 1920, though, and switch the location to a site simultaneously more precise and yet painfully obscure – in fact the provincial city of Norwich in the inter-war years – and the names would be instantly set in stone: Warnes, Burditt, Vinall, Houghton, Murphy. My father was still reciting them to me thirty years after the epic season of 1933–34 in which Norwich won the Division Three (South) championship, along with all manner of other intriguing details, such as the fact that Murphy's nickname was 'Spud' and that a feature of watching the game from the roof of the stand was seeing the light bounce off his bald head. 'Give it to Varco!' my father would sometimes yell humorously across the packed terraces of Carrow Road in the late 1960s (the forward line then was something like Bryceland/Heath/Bolland/ Curran and might it have been Crickmore?) and an elderly man or two would smile regretfully at this summoning up of a long-dead spirit that, forty years before, had roamed unappeasably around a tiny football pitch in North Norwich known as The Nest.

Wander along Riverside, due west from Norwich station towards Mousehold Heath, fetch up in Rosary Road and you can be pretty sure of stumbling upon what was The Nest, although an accumulation of warehousing and office suites has long obliterated any trace of its sporting past. Oddly enough, by holding this book in your hand you are contributing in a small way to The Nest's continuing hold on our lives: Bertram Books, who occupy the site, are one of the UK's largest book wholesalers, and the chances are that a good percentage of the print run spent a week or so reposing on what is now a concrete warehouse floor but seventy years back was a sloping, lop-sided patch of turf that resounded to the cries of the Norfolk faithful. Make no mistake, The Nest was the choicest of soccer grounds. It was a disused chalk pit, with the engaging name of 'Rump's Hole', hastily excavated in the summer of 1908 when the club, then an aspiring Southern League outfit, decided to abandon its cramped quarters on the corner of the Newmarket Road (wood being expensive, the original stand was dismantled piece by piece and carried by horse and cart to its new home).

From the outset, converting this outsize hole in the ground into a functioning soccer venue was an engineer's nightmare. The land starts to rise here towards the heath. Worse, Rosary Road and its adjacent thoroughfares lie smack in the middle of a residential area. Early photographs of the place reflect the improvisational spirit that attended the ground's piecemeal ascent. Along one side of the playing area ran what was known as the 'chicken run' – four solitary rows of seats hemmed in by the backs of the adjoining houses. Down the other side the small covered stand, reassembled after its trip from Newmarket Road, extended for perhaps twenty yards on either side of the halfway line. Most extraordinary of all, though, was the far end – another small stand and then a substantial hill held in place by a concrete restraining wall. From an early stage, Norwich defenders knew they didn't have to bother about – say – a marauding outside right. Provided they could stop him getting the cross in, the man would have to halt well before the touchline to prevent his momentum from slamming him into the concrete.

Late last year the local BBC radio station broadcast an appeal for reminiscences of The Nest. The aim was to interview a dozen or so survivors of this primeval sporting landscape and weave the results into a piece of oral history, helped along by the memories of the presenter – my seventy-seven-year-old father, as it turned out, who attended his first game there (Norwich 0 Fulham 4) in 1929. No one, it should be said, was particularly sanguine about the likely response, if only because the final game played at this odd little mini-amphitheatre was in May 1935. You would have to be seventy, or even seventy-five, to have any coherent memory of even its final days, touching eighty perhaps, to recall 1920s legends like Percy Varco. In the event, these misgivings went unrealised. From across (and in some cases beyond) Norfolk the letters winged in – from spry old gentlemen of ninety who remembered coming up from Suffolk to watch a game in 1923; from blind correspondents dictating to their sons and daughters; from the 1921–22 season club mascot; from a man who claimed to have seen the Sheffield Wednesday 1935 Cup game from the boughs of a tree; from women whose late husbands had 'always supported the City' or had gone themselves in the charge of benevolent uncles. The eldest was a man of ninety-six who saw his first match in 1919.

What did they remember about The Nest, this confidential, garrulous and unfailingly courteous (at least one letter ended with the sign-off 'Yours respectfully') veteran band? More important, perhaps, *how* did they remember it? After all, myth attaches itself just as insidiously, if not more so, to sport as to other branches of human endeavour. Put a collection of eighty- and ninety-year-olds serially in front of a tape-recorder, ask them about an entity as concrete (and at the same time as amorphous) as the history of the local football club, and it is reasonable to expect to see not only the emergence of some kind of collective memory but also something of the mental compost in which that memory takes root and grows. Which is to say that sometimes people called upon to elegise in this way misremem- ber, and that frequently this misremembering is more interesting than accurately recast fact, that what people *believe* happened is often more vital to their sense of themselves, and the community of which they are a part, than what actually did take place.

Inevitably, perhaps, these reminiscences came suffused with an aching nostalgia for a game played by decent young working- class men in front of a decent, familial and predominantly working-class audience, superintended by a club reduced to such depths of penury that it occasionally had to get up sub- scriptions to pay the playing staff's summer wages. Lurking among the accounts of cheery atmospheres, banter with the opposing supporters and the absence of any kind of crowd trouble (a bottle thrown on the pitch in 1935 was as far as hooliganism went in those days, apparently) was a very genuine belief that football had lost something in the intervening sixty years – a loss not just of excitement but of something more intrinsic to itself – and that this forfeiture was the fault of the men in suits. 'I still love City,' an eighty-one-year-old poignantly observed, 'but feel football is not as thrilling as in the old days. Too much money. Too little heart in every game.' One of the great axioms of modern life is that nothing is ever what it was, of course, but one would like to think that many a dollar-eyed Premiership chairman might feel just a twinge of shame if he ever read those words. But then again, why should he? He's giving the people what they want, bless him.

Moving on to The Nest itself, and Norwich City's far from consistent performances therein – they moved up into the old Third Division South in the early 1920s but further glory was a long time coming – people tended to recall three principal events. These were the tumultuous 0–5 FA Cup third round turning over by Corinthians, the country's last decent amateur side, in 1929, the promotion-winning season of 1933–34, and the Sheffield Wednesday FA Cup fifth round showdown of 1935 when they went down 0–1 to a goal by the England international Rimmer. The Wednesday game in particular had a little corner all of its own in these memorial gardens. Nearly all the correspondents had attended it. One old gentleman claimed to have been the first person in the queue outside the St Leonard's Road turnstiles at nine that morning, and to have been cordially greeted by Burditt on his way to early training. Others recalled the huge crowd (variously put at between 20 and 30,000-plus) and the attempts of the thousands left outside to force their way in. Some of them, hopping over from the chalkhill 'Kop', climbed onto the roof of the second stand. Another raiding party sped along the cottage gardens that abetted the chicken run, to the horror of local residents. 'It was like trying to stop the tide coming in,' someone remembered.

Then there were the players. Numerous people had yelled, or claimed to have yelled, 'Give it to Varco!' (Varco was an ox-like centre forward who notched up 47 goals in his 65 appearances). Warnes, Burditt, Vinall, Houghton and Murphy strode like colossi across the Elysian turf, along with the herculean 1920s goalkeeper Charlie Dennington (whose thirteen-stone frame opposing forwards prudently avoided when he rose for a high cross), the future English international Alf Kirchen, and the long-serving right back and club captain Joe Hannah.

However, even these tended to be relegated to the substitutes' bench at the expense of some recurring fragments of folk memory. Chief among these were the recollection that when Norwich scored and the wind was in the right direction you could hear the noise of cheering at St Faith's (a picturesque village several miles out into the Norfolk countryside), and the habit of enterprising householders whose premises overlooked the ground of renting out their back bedrooms on match days. A Mr Weekes, for instance, who cut hair in St Leonard's Road, pursued a kind of double trade by attending to his clients in the front room and then ushering them towards the grandstand view offered by the back of the house.

Working out what to make of this tide of spirited and unquenchably good-natured nostalgia is not as easy as it sounds. To mutter that it isn't *accurate* is beside the point. Determining where memory shades into myth and the reasons for that transfer is rarely straightforward, and while it's not quite true to say that inter-war support for Norwich City necessarily reduces itself to inalienable focus points – Sheffield Wednesday, back rooms to let and Spud Murphy's bald head – it would be correct to say that this kind of communal reflection is often a fair distance from the testimony of the record books. Take, for example, the question of the crowds.

Everybody knew – even women recounting what their husbands had told them – that The Nest attracted big gates, but exactly how big? 20,000? 30,000? In fact, the 20,000-plus attendances were largely confined to big cup games, and the absolute record was 25,057 against Sheffield Wednesday. The *average* number of spectators during the 1933–34 promotion season was a more modest 13,500. Then again, take the question of the players and their hold on the public mind. Almost certainly, many of the people who claimed to have encouraged their team with shouts of 'Give it to Varco!' only think they did so. Even my father never actually saw him, although the records show that he was still on the books at the time of the Fulham game of August 1929.

In much the same way, the giant, roaming monsters of legend have a habit of diminishing in size when set against reference books such as Eastwood and Davage's monumental *Canary Citizens*. Charlie Dennington, certainly, was a Schmeichel-sized six feet plus, but the average height of the 1933–34 forward line was something under five feet nine. Percy Varco's rampages through craven opposition defences must have been accomplished at a fairly sedate pace, as Eastwood and Davage have him down as weighing thirteen stone (for purposes of comparison, West Ham's John Hartson, possibly the beefiest forward in the current Premiership, tips the scales at around fourteen and a half, while standing a good four inches taller). Even the placid, family-oriented character of the ground seems a shade less idyllic when closely inspected. A fence gave way during the Sheffield Wednesday game, the crowd spilled out onto the pitch, and many of the teenage boys present watched the proceedings in a state of terror. 'I was very pleased to get out of that ground after the match,' one remembered. 'I was never so scared at a football match in my life.' Post-Heysel, post-Hillsborough and the fan graveyards of the 1980s, one looks back at the safety arrangements with disbelieving horror. It is a fact, for example, that the boys who toured the perimeter selling chocolate – 'Caley's Marching Chocolate' it was called, made at the local factory – were often reduced to throwing the merchandise up into the terraces and trusting that the money was thrown back. People who fainted in the crush of the Wednesday game were simply passed down to the waiting St John ambulancemen over the heads of the crowd.

There is nothing unusual in the ease with which this kind of debunking can be set in motion. Most of the consolations of past time are illusory, when it comes down to it, and would hardly be consolations if they weren't. And one shouldn't, perhaps, mark down this untangling of fact and something which is a bit less – and at the same time more – than fact as 'debunking', for the myths are rock-solid, as real to several thousand elderly inhabitants of the county of Norfolk as the Norse gods were to the average Viking. *Spud Murphy played better with a drink or two inside him. On a good day you could hear the noise at St Faith's. 30,000 they had there for the Wednesday game.* None of this may be 'true' in the forensic sense, but taken together it represents a collective search for something, something at once communal and faintly elusive, to do with people's idea of themselves, where they lived, the pleasures – shared and solitary – of past time.

Running beneath it, and no less susceptible to some sort of extraction, are several sharp glances at the way in which a minor professional football club conducted its business in the 1920s and 1930s, and the economic conditions in which it operated. Despite cup-runs, 20,000 gates and the occasional bright lad who could be exported to the First Division, Norwich were perennially hard-up. Efforts to make the ground 'pay' as something other than a playing surface – by putting on boxing tournaments or staging dances (a floor was laid in front of the old stand, and the band sat in the stand itself) – habitually failed to work. Meanwhile, a sprawling low-level economy was being kicked into existence, both in and around the ground. Leaving aside the *rentiers* of the St Leonard's Road back-to-backs, there was a lucrative trade in 'minding' bicycles (2d a time) in the front gardens of nearby houses. In this and other ways whole families could find themselves more or less employed by the club and its offshoots. The Hawes family in the early 1920s included a father who functioned as assistant trainer and an elder son, 'Tricky', who was on the playing staff. To supplement these fairly modest receipts, Mrs Hawes washed the team kit each week in the kitchen copper, while seven-year-old Paddy officiated as the club mascot. Nearly eighty years later he remembers sitting in the stand – in those days mascots didn't make it onto the turf – in a miniature version of the strip designed by his mother, and being paid five shillings if Norwich won, half-a-crown if they drew, and nothing at all if they lost.

Anecdotes like this demonstrate how deeply Norwich City and The Nest had managed to embed themselves in local culture and the local economy in the early inter-war era, a bare twenty years after the club's foundation at a venue named the Criterion Café in 1902. So, too, does the testimony of the attendance figures. Norwich is not a populous place. Even now it harbours barely 120,000 inhabitants. Seventy years ago there were a great deal fewer, and yet 20,000 of them could sometimes be persuaded to turn up at a dug-out chalk pit north of the city to watch an inconsistent Third Division side be put through its paces. Without doubt, the existence of a professional football club filled a substantial gap in local leisure pursuits. One can see this most clearly in the distances people were prepared to travel – this at a time when public transport was in its infancy and the Norfolk back-roads were mostly pot-holes – to see a match: from Great Yarmouth, say, twenty miles away on the coast, or Watton in the south-west corner of the county, which is a forty-six-mile round trip, in those days undertaken by bicycle. One correspondent remembered being brought all the way from Woodbridge, in South Suffolk, as an eight-year-old in 1923.

Even at that stage, oddly enough, The Nest was well into the second half of its not very long life. It had always been tacitly accepted that the club would need better facilities if it could ever hope to fulfil its ambitions. Promotion to Division Two in 1934 only confirmed the want of what 'Canary', writing in the *Eastern Daily Press*, called 'adequate room on and around the pitch', and Sheffield Wednesday had prepared for the cup clash by training on a pitch whose extremities had been roped off, the better to mimic the Lilliputian territory of Rosary Road. In fact the era of The Nest began to fade away only a fortnight after the 1935 cup exit. On 1 March City's rising star, Alf Kirchen, was sold to Arsenal for the unimaginable sum of £6,000 (again, for the purposes of comparison, my father's annual wage as a sixteen-year-old office boy at the Norwich Union insurance company in 1937 was a magnificent £45). On 6 May were enacted what turned out to be the place's last rites, when an Arsenal side including Kirchen, Hapgood and Leslie Compton arrived to contest a grand old institution called the Norfolk and Norwich Hospital Cup. Arsenal won 1–0 in front of 15,000 people. A fortnight later came a letter from the FA drawing attention to reports of the ground's unsuitability for large crowds. By the end of May, the board had accepted the offer of a replacement site near Thorpe Station. There followed one of the more remarkable construction feats in football stadium history. Dumping began on what was then the Carrow Road ground of the engineering firm Boulton and Paul's sports club on 11 June; by 17 August the terraces and stand were mostly complete. Carrow Road was opened to the public on 31 August, when 29,779 spectators saw Norwich beat West Ham 4–3.

At which point The Nest, where Charlie Dennington scared the life out of opposing centre forwards and Percy Varco (who later retired to his native West Country, was twice mayor of Fowey and ended up a public figure of some note) charged down timid goalkeepers, falls out of the history books. Presumably amateur games were played there for a while, unregarded by shirt-sleeved locals staring from their back windows, until some sharp-eyed developer ordered up the concrete mix. No one knows; my father, by then in Ireland with the RAF, can't remember. All the same, The Nest's legacy remains – not simply in the photographs of seas of Norwich faces, calm and attentive under flat caps, or the memories of a couple of dozen Norfolk pensioners, but in its implications for the here and now.

To talk about soccer having 'lost' something in the century or so of its professional existence is to ignore a great deal of more or less unignorable reality. Whether we like it or not, association football – that game that you and I played on the park as children, that our dads took us to on bitter afternoons in the dead 1960s – is, like everything else, caught up in the post-modern hurricane of money and instant communications, of things being available *now*, to anyone who feels like paying for them. The choice facing professional soccer in this country is as stark as that confronting the Australian aborigine: either, as the late Shiva Naipaul once put it, he can become the modern citizen of a modern world, or he can retreat into an artificial, state-subsidised playground of jumbucks and *ersatz* cave art. In other words, not really a choice at all. At the same time it is possible to be both the modern citizen of a modern world and to remember that your ancestors foraged over the outback. Pure, blind soccer nostalgia is as dreary as any attempt to embalm the past without troubling to ask what it was that the past actually consisted of, and even the most elegiac fan can sometimes feel slightly jaundiced at the prospect of having to read the kind of books reviewed in the fanzines which have titles like *Non-league football grounds of the West Midlands*. In heritage, as in everything else, there is a duty to discriminate, to take what seems important to joint and single identities, and to jettison the rest. And yet there is a sense in which a game deprived of its roots – of the social and historical framework that made it what it was – becomes merely an entertainment. One doesn't have to be a Fulham fan, for example, to find something faintly obscene in the spectacle of Mohammed Al Fayed striding out onto the turf of Craven Cottage. Not, heaven help us, because Al Fayed is sometimes seen as a seedy Egyptian businessman, but because of his complete spiritual detachment from the thing he owns. A hundred and fifty years ago, a rich man trying to advance himself in national society would have bought himself a seat in Parliament: nowadays he has to settle for a Second Division football club.

Going back to the brief, imperfectly recalled, history of The Nest, one finds something that, however cursorily, gave pattern to thousands of individual lives, that was remembered not so much for what it was, as for what it was thought or desired to be, a stage on which individual appearances immediately gain a context. One of the radio interviewees, for instance, remembered a Good Friday game during which news came over the tannoy that Mussolini had invaded Albania, and that King Zog had disappeared. Good Friday! Mussolini! King Zog! All of a sudden a kind of window is opened up onto past time – a vista which is both football and something more than football and from which neither part is detachable – something from which, thankfully, the Al Fayeds and their sidekicks are eternally debarred. It is important to remember these prosaic origins, if only because of their ability to tether the game not among the depredations of the soccer plutocrats, million-pound salaries and the antics of Murdoch's satellite hooligans but amid countless individual lives. The Nest shut a quarter of a century before I was born, but I can never look at the photographs of those cloth-capped multitudes, the old women with their favours and the soapbox-toting children, all the dead, good-natured and somehow *decent* faces, without experiencing a queer twinge of recognition. Sixty years later, borne from another world, they are still a part of my life, and what living in Norfolk entails, as vital to me in some odd way, as my parents' faces seen across the tablecloth, or the gaudy tops of the Norwich market stalls shimmering in the rain.

The author would like to thank Matthew Gudgin, John Taylor and David Clayton for their help in preparing this article. The Nest *was first broadcast on BBC Radio Norfolk on 26 December 1997.*

desperately seeking euclid

NICHOLAS ROYLE

These days, if you happen to be a middle-class writer with more than half a brain who chooses to write about football, you can't do so without some *Observer* paperback reviewer giving you a hard time for desperately seeking Euclid. Any description of the action which goes beyond 'He kicked the ball from A to B' is deemed to be invoking the spirit of the great Greek father of geometry.

Well, four months ago a lad called Johnny Euclid started playing for our team, so does that give me the right? Does that let me off the hook?

It wasn't his real name, of course.

His real name was Vangelis Euclid.

You can see why he had to change it. One slow-motion run down the right wing in his baggy shorts and the opposition defenders were breaking into a ragged chorus of 'Chariots of Fire'. They all knew his name; everybody knew everybody else's name; there were only four teams in the 'league'. Four teams of eight men each, rotating Sunday evening fixtures. We played for an hour at either six or eight o'clock.

'Der da da da der der,' they went, 'der da da da der.'

And Johnny would grin indulgently, good-naturedly, accepting the joke as you would a pat on the back, like Tim Robbins wandering back from the latrine in the Vietnam scene at the beginning of *Jacob's Ladder* – they even looked a little alike. But he wouldn't let it put him off his stride. Instead he'd deliver another inch-perfect looping cross to the back post where Danny would meet it with his high intellectual forehead (mind you, I can't talk). Pick that one out.

It didn't matter whether it was Danny, or Simon or Tony, Johnny Euclid always flighted in the perfect cross so that the finishing touch simply *was* a matter of geometry. The forward would have to trip over and fall flat on his face not to score. The strength of Johnny Euclid's game lay in its inevitability, its faultless structure. Its . . . geometry – okay?

Generally, not that much was known about him off the field, his pattern being to turn up just before kick-off, play his normal, vastly superior game, then vanish in the vague direction of Shepherd's Bush. I'd shared a beer with him at the Station Tavern one night after a particularly emphatic victory. On a second occasion I'd bumped into him in a sports shop on the Uxbridge Road. He'd been looking for new shin pads. I per-suaded him to come for a drink with me, and once I got him into the Andover Arms with a couple of beers inside him it was hard to shut him up.

Atom Ergün cast a final look around his room to check he hadn't forgotten anything. The poster on the wall advertising his namesake Atom Egoyan's movie *Exotica* was drifting free at one corner and beginning to curl up. The black and white photo-graph of the 1954 Turkey World Cup squad over his desk was framed, therefore not susceptible to adhesive-fatigue. He reflected again, as he did every time he looked at it, that it was a great shame his father had never actually got to play in his national side's finest hour, food poisoning having forced him out of the squad at the last minute.

All Atom could offer by way of tribute to his father was his weekly Sunday evening run-out for the Harringay Harriers at the Westway Sports Centre. Not that his father could very easily come to watch. Having emigrated to Britain after the disappointment of 1954, Atom's parents settled in north London, where their first son was born in 1974 and Atom followed four years later. As soon as Atom got his place at Oxford, mother and father returned to Turkey, where they hoped the two boys would one day follow them.

Most students, of course, went up to London at the weekend and returned to Oxford on Sunday night. Atom bucked the trend so that he could still make his regular game; there was also the fact he didn't have any lectures before Thursday, and his brother's place on one of the lower rungs of the Harringay ladder offered more comfort than Atom's Cowley Road bedsit.

The only time another side to Johnny Euclid's character would emerge was on the occasions when the Harringay Harriers, one of the teams we took on every other week or so, played their star striker, Atom Ergün.

Every so often there would be a player you didn't care for, some kid you might take against. Irrationally or otherwise. In my own case, there was the tall blond lad who played for the White Shirts.

Blondie was of the old school of attacking thought. He certainly hadn't read the new FIFA directives on not kicking the shit out of the goalkeeper. The ball – a lovely, looping, perfectly flighted ball, I had to admit – was heading for the top corner, but there was a chance that with a correctly timed leap in that direction I might tip it over the bar or around the post. I was aware of Blondie piling in all the while. I leapt. There was sufficient contact between glove and ball to tip it over and concede a corner and then there was sufficient contact between Blondie and myself for him to wrap my body around the goal post.

Hurt, but not so badly that I couldn't speak, I raged at him.

Two simple words sufficed, but I bellowed them. I'm frankly a bit of a shortarse for a goalkeeper, so my outburst was pretty surprising, especially to such a hulking monster, but he didn't come near me again. Until the end of the game.

It was not uncommon that a ball got kicked up on to the roundabout. The pitch was an oblong of Astroturf dropped into the middle of the roundabout where the M41, or West Cross Route, joined the Westway in west London. Down one side of the pitch ran the Westway itself, straight as an arrow, and at sufficient altitude not to be a problem. Some guy had once kicked the ball high enough, but thankfully had failed to get any direction on it – the ball hit the underside of one of the deck sections and bounced straight back down. But the other three sides of the pitch were bordered by half of the elevated round-about. It was not quite as high off the ground as the Westway and the ball actually went up there perhaps twice a month. Sometimes it would go right over and fall back into the street outside the New Latimer Arms. On other occasions it would hit the road surface, somehow missing all the vehicles which were invariably present, and bounce over the edge and back down. But usually it disappeared. We listened, or we covered our ears and eyes in horror, but we never heard the expected impact. The catastrophic, Ballardian event we all expected did not occur. Somehow. By some freak of luck it simply didn't happen. Or it hadn't happened yet.

But, mysteriously, the ball would disappear. If you took your car up on to the roundabout after the game, there was no sign of the ball, despite the enclosed space. We couldn't explain it. Although I don't suppose all the lads were as bothered by it as I undoubtedly was.

During this same game against the White Shirts, someone kicked the ball up on to the roundabout and it didn't reappear. We had a spare ball – mine – which I lobbed upfield so that a throw-in could be taken and the game resumed.

Seconds later the guys who were on next started trooping in by the gate in the bottom corner. Funny how they never waited, never even let us carry on until the ball went out of play. But at the beginning of our allotted hour, whatever time we happened to be playing, the previous lot would always take an age to wrap up and get off the field.

The game was over, so I headed for the far end of the pitch to reclaim my ball. Blondie wouldn't give it to me, however. 'One of your lot kicked my ball on to the motorway,' he said.

Now I started to like him a lot less.

I considered the various options open to me and took the stupidest.

'Well, that's a shame, but it's your bad luck and now I'm going to take my ball.'

'Fuck off.'

I felt that he was less entitled to speak in this manner than I had been earlier, and sensed that discussion was pointless, so I simply bent down and picked the ball up from his feet. Why he didn't hit me I'll never know, because he was certainly the type.

Anyway, I'd taken against him.

I also took against a guy in another game who kicked very hard in the general direction of the ball while I was actually holding it. He sprained my finger ligament so badly it put me out of action for several weeks. It wasn't the kick itself so much as his lack of an apology and the fact I had to strain to hear his muttered self-justification: 'I had to go for it.'

No you didn't, actually. You didn't have to go for it at all.

The fact that the White Shirts couldn't come up with a better name was perhaps symptomatic of a flawed team spirit – they disbanded soon after the lost-ball incident and I've never seen Blondie again.

Johnny Euclid, meanwhile, had taken against Atom Ergün.

Whenever we played the Harriers, and Atom was playing, Johnny would be bad-tempered and irritable. 'Fucking Turkish bastard,' I heard him grumble on more than one occasion. 'Should fuck off back to Turkey.'

'Johnny,' I remarked, 'I think he was born in Tottenham.'

Whenever a shot from Atom went wide or over the bar, Johnny would shout 'Nineteen fifty-four' or 'Seven-two'. The first time I heard these remarks, they seemed strangely meaningless, until Gav, a half-Norwegian sound engineer and our captain, explained that 1954 was the year Turkey had last featured in the World Cup finals and that 7–2 was the result of their play-off game against West Germany – in West bloody Germany's favour, naturally. Turkey had not progressed beyond the group stage.

But Greece, I knew, had hardly covered themselves in glory in USA 94.

'Played three, won none, drawn none, lost three,' Atom happily reminded Johnny. 'Goals for – none; goals against – ten. Points – none. Bottom of the group. Don't know why they even bothered turning up.'

At the time, it seemed a little odd that mere Greek-Turkish rivalry should provoke such animosity between the two of them, but I for one knew it was slightly more complicated than perhaps Atom was aware of. When Johnny and I had that post-match beer in the Station Tavern, one of the things that came out in conversation was that Johnny was actually a Greek Cypriot, his father a Cypriot diplomat in London. Johnny and his younger brother, Lambros, had been born and initially raised on the island where they had befriended several children living on the other side of the Green Line. About once a month they would organise a game of football on a patch of wasteground on the edge of the city. One particular Sunday, in the heat, a Turkish soldier had run amok firing his automatic weapon indiscriminately.

The soldier had apparently shown signs of being depressed for some time, the Turkish authorities later said by way of apology, without saying sorry.

His action had fatally injured one of the boys playing football.

'My brother Lambros,' said Johnny. 'He was twelve.'

Whatever the speed and quality of the game, being in goal gave me the best position from which to observe its ebb and flow. I could see the lines of attack being opened and then reopened.

I believe I can even see the lines of energy criss-crossing the field. When Johnny Euclid makes a run down the right wing, he scorches the air around him. The ball is passed into space ahead of him and he meets it without having to alter his stride, right foot striking the ball, sending it curling over to the back post where even now Danny is rising above the defence so he can knock it down, on target, giving the keeper no chance.

In real life Danny is some kind of therapist. On the field he's a loose-ball therapist. No loose ball sits around feeling lonely for long when Danny's playing.

If it's a slow game or a viscous, frustrating midfield tussle, I'll divert my attention to the lines of energy around the pitch – there's the Westway itself sweeping overhead, the West Cross Route along which traffic races up from the Holland Park roundabout to join the Westway; there's the elevated round-about, receiving traffic from the West Cross Route heading into town as well as vehicles which have come off the Westway in order to proceed down the West Cross Route to the Holland Park roundabout. From where we are we can't see much on the Westway; we just hear an ambient murmur from overhead. On the roundabout we see the upper parts of any high-sided vehicles such as ambulances, trucks, fire engines and the Oxford Tube, the coach service between London and Oxford.

In addition there's the nearby overground tube line between Shepherd's Bush and Latimer Road. Closer and indeed clearly visible from the pitch is a Railtrack line carrying the occasional goods train and, snaking elegantly through the silvery darkness, yellow and blue Eurostar trains returning to the depot for the night.

It's impossible not to believe this intricate, intersecting pattern of energy lines has some effect on our game.

Atom preferred the Oxford Tube to the train into Paddington. It was cheaper than the train and, if he was going straight to a game, he could get off opposite the Kensington Hilton then take a short walk up St Ann's Road and Bramley Road, parallel with the West Cross Route, and reach the sports centre with plenty of time to change before the game.

He always sat on the right-hand side of the coach by the window. A student of human geography at Keble with a special interest in public transport, Atom liked to get the best possible view of the tube station at Hillingdon – as far as he was concerned, the finest piece of modern architecture in or around the capital. His best friend at college, James, said if he wanted to study architecture he should have gone to a different university, since it was one of the subjects Oxford didn't offer. Atom remarked to James that he wasn't aware of Oxford offering courses in doing lots of drugs and going to millions of raves either, but that was what James seemed to spend most of his time doing.

Atom liked the clean lines of Hillingdon, the deceptive simplicity. It looked far more complex than it actually was. Each ride past it on the Oxford Tube refined his appreciation of the construction.

The previous week, as the coach swept by the tube station, Atom had thought it could be said to resemble his love life, in that it looked intricate and complex but was actually very straightforward. This week, granted another look at its white girders and glassy perforations, he wasn't so sure: his situation was more tangled than he had liked to admit.

Even if he hadn't known the identity of Sarah's boyfriend when he had started seeing her as well, he knew he shouldn't have got involved. Now that he *did* know exactly whose girlfriend he had been sleeping with for the last six months, there was little sense in his continuing to run the risk that the cuckold would find out.

But, if Johnny were to be put in possession of the facts, life would surely become very unpleasant indeed.

Johnny Euclid was on fire. So far, this was the best performance I had seen from him. He wasn't just making the runs and delivering the crosses; his running off the ball was imaginative and unselfish, and his darting through the midfield with the ball then releasing it to one of our lads coming up behind was giving Rain Tree Crew a major headache. We were five-nil up and only twenty minutes into the game.

Johnny had scored one of the goals, a simple tap-in from an indirect free-kick after their keeper had handled a back-pass. The others had been shared equally between Danny and Stu, both of whom were sparking off Johnny and fizzing with energy. The defence – Dave, Dave and Gav – was solid and hardworking, constantly checking back; and the midfield, Stu and James, worked tirelessly in the middle of the park, allowing the whole team to mesh like a well-oiled cliché.

And for twenty minutes I had managed to keep a clean sheet. Clearly this was thanks mainly to the efforts of Dave, Dave and Gav, but I was still giving myself a small pat on the back. As any attacker with the ball at his feet who has ever faced me knows, I am not a natural born keeper: five foot seven, short-sighted and if I know anything at all about football, it's only what I've picked up watching the game. The team I used to play for introduced training sessions. That's why they're the team I *used* to play for.

We – the Kensal Risers – have our own way of psyching ourselves up to win. In the tense few seconds before kick-off one of the lads will lead the team in a round of 'pointless clapping'.

But no one is actually more enthusiastic than I am. No one looks forward to the game more than I do, and no one regrets the sound of the final whistle quite as much. I just love the game. I love being part of a team and I love playing in goal and shouldering the particular responsibility that entails. I've never kept a clean sheet, but at the level we play, scorelines are always high and no one really cares if we win or lose. Sure we play to win, but if we lose we lose and once we're off the park we've forgotten about it. We don't even have post-match autopsies. And because we don't stop for half-time, we don't have to stand around saying meaningless things like 'There's this massive space in front of Dave' or 'If Danny moves across and Si drops back, Tony'll be able to capitalise on the first-time balls'. Given five minutes with nothing else to do, we'd be unable to resist the temptation.

Despite the fact everyone professes to be not that bothered, we all secretly are, of course, and a clean sheet is a major priority. One which I never expect to achieve, but which is always my goal, as it were. I know the lads would rather go home with a win under their belts, helped along by a little pointless clapping. It will get them through the rest of the evening without snapping at whoever's waiting at home; they may even get up and do the 3 a.m. feed.

So why am I not happy when the ball is up the other end? When we are nearer to scoring a goal than the possibility of conceding one? Why do I silently will James to lose it in midfield and urge the Rain Tree Crew striker to take a long-range pot-shot at my top corner?

James loses it. The Rain Tree striker looks up, telling me exactly where the ball is going – or where he thinks it's going. He makes contact. I'm unsighted for a split second, but I knew where it was going so I dive, and turn it around for a corner.

'Save, keeper.'

'Nice one.'

Stu claps me on the back.

'Great stuff.'

That's why.

That's why I prefer it when the ball's down our end.

A high-sided removal van lumbers around the roundabout heading for the West Cross Route.

It's odd, but when you score a goal you run around and celebrate and you can smile and grin and look goofy and everyone expects it of you. But if you're a keeper and you pull off a good save, you just get on with it. Somehow it feels uncool even to acknowledge the comments of your team-mates.

Johnny's in space – but then he always is. I side-foot the ball out to him. He controls it and flicks it behind one of Rain Tree Crew's eager ringers to where Stu has made a run, and off we go again. Stu works in sound archiving. He's certainly a sound midfielder.

A Eurostar train intrudes its sleek snout into the space between one of the Westway's concrete stanchions and the high metal fence that borders our pitch.

Stu knocks it back to Johnny, and Johnny immediately digs his toe under the ball, chipping the keeper from thirty yards.

Any minute now, the Oxford Tube will arrive at the round-about and make its way slowly around – every week as regular as clockwork, in the dying minutes of the game.

Six-nil.

★ ★ ★

That time when I bumped into Johnny on the Uxbridge Road in Parksy's and we headed down into Brackenbury Village to get a pint at the Andover Arms, he seemed at first as if he was just being polite. I was aware that he probably thought I was tugging his arm, but the man intrigued me. How old was he? Twenty-two, twenty-three? None of us really knew. He looked young and I knew he was doing a PhD at Oxford. Something to do with maths.

The Andover Arms kept Newcastle Brown, for some convoluted reason Johnny's beer of choice, and they served it the way the brewer recommends – very cold in a half-pint glass which you can then keep topped up. After we'd got through one of these each, I asked Johnny about his PhD and he told me, but I'm buggered if I can remember the first thing about it, other than he needed to know a fuck of a lot about geometry. Which of course he did.

'You're a keeper,' he said, once he'd returned from the bar with another round.

I gave him a puzzled look.

'Are you a good keeper?'

'Am I a good keeper? What kind of a question is that? Of course not. I'm a shit keeper, but I enjoy it, and every now and then I stop the ball going in the net.'

'No, no, you misunderstand me.' He knocked back half a glass. 'Are you a good keeper of *other* things? Can you, for instance, keep a secret?'

He must have perhaps had a couple of beers before we'd got together. His words were beginning to run into one another. Or maybe he just couldn't take his ale.

'Yes, I can keep a secret. Discretion's my middle name.'

'Funny you should say that, because my name's not what you think it is, not what *everyone* thinks it is.'

'I know, I know. It's Vangelis rather than Johnny. We've always known that. Tell me something we don't know.'

'No, no,' he said, wiping his hand across his mouth and pouring more Newcastle Brown into his glass. 'Euclid is not my real name. It's just a nickname I've had since I came over here with my dad, 'cause I was good at maths and 'cause of where I'm from, you know?'

'Right. So what's your real name then?'

'Karapapas.'

'Karapapas?'

'Karapapas. Vangelis Karapapas.' He lifted his glass to mine. 'But you can call me Johnny Euclid.'

'Right.'

Later – several Newcastle Browns later – he leaned across the table towards me and said, 'Hey keeper, can you keep a secret?'

'I thought we'd already done that, Johnny,' I said.

He shook his head, grinning. 'That wasn't really a secret. Not a big secret. Do you wanna know my big secret?'

I nodded. I mean, I wasn't that bothered, but if he wanted to confide in me —

'Do you believe in the perfect murder?'

'The perfect murder presumably being one in which the murderer doesn't get found out?'

His turn to nod.

I said: 'I don't know if I do believe in the perfect murder.'

'I do,' he said, draining his glass for the hundredth time. 'Must be my analytical mind. My maths training.'

'Yes, I suppose from the murderer's point of view, an unsolved murder is neater than a solved murder. It's a better outcome for the murderer, who after all is the only person who knows the solution. He's solved the murder by committing it, really. I think.' I was beginning to get my thoughts muddled up somewhat by this point.

'But if the police can't solve it, it's not very satisfying for them, is it? So then it's hardly the perfect murder.'

'You're confusing the issue, keeper. Who cares about the police? Who cares about the victim? Or *victims*, for that matter? The murderer only cares about one person. And if he gets away with it, then it's the perfect murder.'

Under the Hanger Lane gyratory, past Park Royal tube, easing up for the lights at Savoy Circus.

Atom checked his bag. He was going to be getting off at the Kensington Hilton and walking up for his eight o'clock game. They were playing Red Star Kilburn, which meant that the Kensal Risers would be playing Rain Tree Crew, having kicked off at six, so they'd still be on now and close to finishing. Atom knew that Johnny Euclid tended to disappear after a game rather than hang around and shower or anything, but still he decided to take it slowly up St Ann's Road and Bramley Road. No point running into trouble.

He didn't know how much longer he could live with the worry, the duplicity. It was harder for Sarah, of course, who was still technically going out with Johnny. But Atom wasn't keen on confrontation.

He should never have started it. He should never even have gone to the Oxford Union that day. What was he thinking of? A Turk, a north London working-class Turk at that, turning up at the Oxford Union for the debate – this house believes that Turkey has no place in Cyprus – when practically everyone else there was either white middle-class intellectual (like Sarah) or wealthy Greek (like Johnny).

She was gorgeous though. That was the thing. And put like that, it seemed simple.

He saw her first in the bar, trotted out some line about a girl sitting alone with an empty glass.

'My boyfriend's just gone upstairs to the library,' she said.

'Then have a drink with me until he gets back,' he said, and he'd caught the bartender's eye before she'd had a chance to refuse. She accepted the drink – he was a good-looking, hazel-eyed boy – but strongly advised he leave *before* the boyfriend got back.

'See you in the debate then,' he said, getting up to go five minutes later. As he headed for the door, a postgrad student he vaguely recognised from around college swept past him. Atom turned to look back and saw Sarah smile at the newcomer, but it was a half-guilty, self-conscious smile, and Atom knew he'd made an impression.

And that was six months ago.

They bore left off the Westway and Atom looked out of the window as the coach rolled down to the roundabout. Once the road was clear and the driver had pulled out into the right-hand lane, Atom had a perfect view of the pitch, like when they switched to the aerial shot of Wembley during the Cup final. He saw the little guy in glasses who kept goal for the Kensal Risers standing at the edge of his area. There was no one else in that half of the field. Johnny Euclid, on the right wing, was in a good position to receive the ball. Dave had seen this and laid it off to him. Johnny started his run while the ball was still in motion, collecting it with his left foot and switching it to his right.

Atom swivelled in his seat so he could follow the game. Once the coach got to behind Rain Tree Crew's goal, which was still five or six seconds away, he wouldn't be able to see any more.

Johnny looked up, played a short pass to Stu and continued his run, obviously looking for a one-two. Stu didn't disappoint him. There were a couple of forwards running into space at the back post, arms raised, but the way Johnny ran at the ball now, Atom guessed he was going for a shot. He certainly wasn't expecting what did happen next.

'it's ok. i'm with gary lineker'

MARCELA MORA Y ARAUJO

Gary Lineker was born one 30 November thirty-seven years ago, the son of a Leicester market-stall owner who wished he'd been a footballer. While Gary's brother got himself in and out of trouble, Gary was bright and disciplined, good at maths, and would probably have gone on to do 'A' levels and even university if he hadn't turned out such a natural goalscorer – by far the most lucrative skill a young man can hope for. When he was sixteen years old, one Jon Holmes entered his life, and together they have since worked with impeccable proficiency towards turning Mr Lineker into one of the highest earning sports celebrities in the kingdom. Unlike other ex-football players, Lineker sheds no tears for his playing years: the training was always a drag. With that cheeky smile which is now tantamount to a logo for Walkers Salt 'n' Lineker flavoured product he states: 'I'm not a football player; I'm a crisps salesman.'

But there was a time when he *was* a football player. As such, his biggest achievement was without a doubt the 1986 World Cup in Mexico, where his six goals during the tournament earned him a trophy invented by the sportswear manufacturer Adidas – an otherwise standard boot covered in gold plate and aptly known as a Golden Boot. Just reward for a performance on behalf of his queen and country which saw him score 48 goals in 80 appearances for En-Ger-Land, second only to Bobby Charlton. True, in '86 all six goals came from within ten yards and took a maximum of two touches – mathematical, economic,

Saxon football, very removed from more romantic notions of a number ten's performance. Lineker himself is the first to admit they were all 'goal-hangers'. They lacked the balletic qualities of more Latin-style number tens, those described both sides of the River Plate as 'the thinkers, the players who can pause'. They were not memorable goals in the way that, say, other goals of the same World Cup were. People don't sit around bars and cafés all over the world saying: 'You know England–Argentina in '86, you know Lineker's header in the second half, now there's a goal I've always wished I'∂ scored.' People the world over haven't rioted en masse, or committed collective suicide, or discovered religion, or believed in miracles because of *that* goal. The history of football isn't now widely regarded as before and after *that* goal. But that goal was a decider of sorts, and it was number six for the only player whose list got that far. At the end of the day it's the result that counts, and the Golden Boot Trophy was awarded to Gary Lineker, now OBE. In an otherwise superbly accurate piece published in *Living Marxism*, Issue 70, August 1994 Eddie Veal unkindly remarks that 'Lineker won the Golden Boot by scoring six goals but nobody outside his native Leicester remembers any of them.' As it happens, this is not true.

When Gary Lineker OBE set foot in South America once more, on 3 June 1997, he did so as an extremely high-profile VIP. Whether or not this came as a surprise to him remains a mystery, but the fact of the matter is he arrived in Argentina – the first South American port of call in a tour of the world courtesy of the English licence-fee payer – to shoot a documentary series about fellow 'Golden Boots' and found himself to be a celebrity of the most respectable sort. Lineker's own Golden Boot came about because of a goal he scored against Argentina in one mother of a game: few Argentinians don't remember every minute of that England v Argentina encounter and most admire Lineker as a result. Freud might say it helps ease the guilt. It's possible that his obvious hunger for the goal, in such stark contrast to his apparent lack of interest for the game, also appeals.

'You can change your wife or your girlfriend but you can't change your club,' they say in Argentina. Football is popular among the nation as a whole, particularly so among the more marginal masses. Whereas the lawyers and the bankers read the sports section of the paper first on a Monday morning, they have the rest of the paper to relate to as well, but for a substantial section of the Argentine population, the one that constitutes the bulk of the football consumers, only the sports pages exist. In the poorer areas, in the backstreets and the slums, where it's impossible to conceive of providing each child with a toy of their own, a single ball becomes the centre of fun and activity for up to forty kids at a time. Not necessarily a *football*. Any ball. It needn't be a posh branded one. A bunch of old cloths will do. 'Kids don't learn to play football,' says Juan Sasturain, one of Argentina's most original sportswriters, 'they learn to play "ball". The name "football" is wrong because it's not a game you play with your feet – it's a game you *don't* play with your hands.' And all over the city landscapes little boys will balance the ball on their pectorals, bounce it off their shoulders, roll it down their biceps, catch it with their knee and flip it back up to their forehead. Every once in a while one little boy from the slum will prove so uniquely magnificent at 'playing ball' that he will be able to use his shoulder-blades and inner shins with the same dexterity with which most mortals can only use their right hand to scribble their own signature. And all his dreams will come true.

Diego Maradona was born thirty-seven years ago one 30 October, the son of a poverty-stricken couple for whom he was one of eight children. When they realised what their kid could do with a ball, Mr and Mrs Maradona can only have assumed that some sort of divine intervention was at play. For that skinny tiny child's superhuman ability to 'play ball' with his entire body was their ticket out of that hell. They lived in a slum and Diego's mastery of the ball soon became the sole focus of his attention, so school attendance was the exception rather than the rule and whether or not he was any good at maths we don't know. It's unlikely he would have completed primary school anyway, even if he hadn't been good at football, and his chances of attending high school or university were probably as small as his chances of visiting the moon. With time, he would be awarded a diploma from Oxford University – but a made-up one: Master Inspirer of Dreams. (Gary Lineker, on the other hand, has two Honorary MAs, one from Loughborough and one from Leicester University, respectively, both perfectly legit.)

Maradona's exact positioning in the collective psyche of the Argentine nation is in itself worthy of lengthy volumes of analysis. From God to political manoeuvrer, from saint to Machiavellian drug dealer, from villain to victim and back, the whole range of possible interpretations has been covered some-where along the line by the existing literature. A wonderful defi-nition has been provided by Sasturain who argued: 'Maradona is not an interpreter, he is a creator – someone who takes an art or a form such as a game and converts it into something else: invents things that weren't there before.'

Before Gary Lineker arrives in Buenos Aires, Maradona is enjoying a brief retreat from football preparing himself for a 'return' to the game, coincidentally scheduled for the day of Mr Lineker's departure from the country. Signed to local club Boca Juniors (the 'people's club' which boasts as its supporters 'half plus one of the population'), Maradona has not in actual fact been in a fit state to play professional football for some time. Maradona is under contract to America TV to whom he is greatly in debt as they have paid him handsomely for exclusive rights on certain footballing activities, many of which he has not been able to fulfil. The TV station has him by the balls. Maradona is due to start co-hosting his own chat show together with a TV celebrity called Mauro Viale. The latter's existing show broke all ratings records several months before when Maradona and his agent/best friend and right-hand man, Guillermo Coppola, became the protagonists of a tale of sex, drugs, prostitutes and corrupt judges. Mr Viale duly aired everyone's side of the story, and his live daily broadcasts often included scenes of teenage junkie girls pulling each other by the hair and accusing each other of being the grass, the dealer and/or the whore. Coppola did a stint in prison on account of some cocaine allegedly found in his apartment, later said to have been planted there by the girls. In January 1997, having spent three months in prison, he was released because the evidence incriminating the investigating judge and the police in charge of the case was so overwhelming. He was driven straight from his cell to appear live on Mauro Viale's show.

At the TV studios on Maradona's first day as co-host, hundreds of people cram in behind the cameras to watch, among them Natalia Farjat, one of the young ladies mentioned above. 'That's the bird that sent me to jail,' Coppola says, pointing towards her with his chin. It is rumoured she is now Maradona's lover. But then again, it is rumoured that anything that moves is or has been or has the potential to become Maradona's lover.

The very next day Gary Lineker arrives in Buenos Aires. He has been invited onto a peak-time live discussion show hosted by a handful of football players, Maradona not among them. Peak time in Buenos Aires is 11 p.m. Lineker has landed at dawn that morning after a twelve-hour flight from across the other side of the world. At 6 a.m. the following day he is to start his own shooting schedule. Mr Lineker goes straight from breakfast to the golf practice range, then scoffs generous helpings of a traditional Argentine pudding, which consists mostly of a thick sweet milk known locally as Dulce de Leche – together with the bus and the Bic biro one of the great inventions Argentines claim for themselves. In the evening he inquires politely whether he will need to wear a suit and emerges ready for the cameras with his best smile. He discusses topical football matters in Spanish live on national television well into the small hours. On the panel are two players who played against Lineker in Mexico, Burruchaga and Ruggieri. Before going on air – in the Buenos Aires green room – Ruggieri, Lineker's marker in 1986, laughingly tells him how Bilardo had at the time offered him a little 'incentive' of $2000 if he prevented Lineker from scoring. Lineker is visibly flattered; Ruggieri proves to be the first exception to the notion that 'nobody outside [Lineker's] native Leicester remembers' his goals; that header cost him two grand. (When Lineker later hears the story again, this time from Bilardo himself, he laughs and is quick to reply, in Spanish: 'You owe me, I saved you two grand.')

'It was a football programme where they didn't talk at all about football,' Lineker remarks later. The previous weekend a youth had been murdered after violent confrontations among the fans. Violence is currently the number-one problem in Argentine football (some notorious gang leaders have been sentenced to up to thirteen years on charges of 'illicit association', a spurious label previously only applied to combat terrorism, but in spite of this the uncontrolled and random violence among supporters continues, and the death toll rises with it). It is difficult to host a topical football programme on a Tuesday night when an eighteen-year-old has been killed at the stadium on the Sunday and not dwell on the matter. 'They had to talk about violence,' says Lineker, who is a man who understands the television business. But you can tell he feels there wasn't enough talk about *football* anyway. By which one can only assume he means there wasn't enough talk about *tactics*, or *results*.

The following day Gary Lineker travels to Rosario, a city 300 kilometres away from Buenos Aires. Everywhere in Argentina is poorer than the city of Buenos Aires, but Rosario will be Lineker's only taste of anywhere else. The van drives along the totally flat motorway through a landscape which can seem dull but inspired Bruce Chatwin to write one of his most memorable travel books. It enters the Rosario suburbs skirting along abandoned railways and vacant lots where scruffy ragged children 'play ball' between makeshift goalposts. This is Lineker's first sight of the poverty of the shanty town, and his eyes are firmly fixed on what's going on outside the van as they drive along. He remarks, almost to himself: 'So football really is the only thing these people have to hold on to.' Inside the van, the crew are asleep.

He is supposed to do a link by the Arroyito river in Rosario, a river which flows down from the Amazon basin itself and which runs just outside the Rosario Central stadium (also known as the Giant from Arroyito for obvious reasons). He feels uncomfortable. 'I'm not Clive James or Michael Palin,' he reflects. 'I'm still learning.' He feels more at ease delivering cues in a studio and prefers to talk only about football.

He's come to Rosario to interview another Golden Boot winner, Mario Kempes. In this stadium during the 1978 World Cup, Kempes and Argentina beat Peru 6–0 before going on to win the tournament.

On the morning that Gary Lineker and England were to meet Argentina in Mexico '86, the *Sunday Times* broke a story alleging that in '78 Argentina had bribed Peru in order to win by a difference of at least four goals – they needed the points to go through to the next round. Some people see this, and the fact that a military government was in power at the time, as rendering Argentina's first World Cup triumph less than glorious.

Kempes's stock reply has always been: 'There's a whole load of issues that if we had even begun to think about we wouldn't have got past the first round.' Bribe or no bribe, Argentina's luck turned when once in Rosario they met the Peruvians wrapped up in blankets because they were so cold. This was Kempes's club before his move to Valencia in 1976, and at this stadium (also known as the second Chocolate Box, the first one being the Boca Juniors stadium in Buenos Aires), he and the rest of the national squad felt the warmth of the crowd more than in the wider, more modern Monumental stadium which was their home turf in BA. Kempes scored his first two goals of the finals. Three games and four goals later, he too would be crowned Golden Boot winner. He too would get the chance to make a few hundred bucks for the bother of telling his story, twenty years on.

Of the twenty clubs comprising the Argentine first division, fourteen are based in the province of Buenos Aires. For a club like Rosario in the 'interior' of the country – Buenos Aires is that little tummy that sticks out and the rest of the country is therefore considered to be 'inside' – local heroes of the calibre of Kempes don't come ten to the dozen. Whenever he returns to the Giant from Arroyito the staff greet him affectionately. On this particular occasion he and some of the guys find time to share a 'mate' – a strong South American tea – in a tiny office just off the car park, exchanging gossip about the club's current financial straits and fruitless search for an adequate manager. 'It would be so great if you came back,' they say honestly.

Kempes could do with a job, but he knows he's largely outside the circuit of ex-players who get jobs as managers. He's not a natural networker nor a corporate climber. He played football all his life, although he had a few stints as player/manager – Indonesia first, then swapped for what sounded a better offer in Albania only to find, barely a few weeks after his arrival, that his new employer was one of the businessmen who had set up the pyramid schemes. Kempes was evacuated as things got hairy and, under contract still, has been spending the last year staying with his parents and his brother in his home town of Bellville. His ex-wife and their three children still live in Valencia, where Kempes spent most of his professional life. Now he travels to Buenos Aires on Saturdays, where he has a part-time job kicking penalties on some TV show, but Kempes loves to play and as manager would often include himself in the squad even if he would take himself off the pitch when he got tired. Aged forty-one. He knows what the deal is in the appointment of managers, he knows he's not in the running for Rosario, or any other first division club for that matter. But he smiles, touched by the thought.

And as he leads Gary Lineker, one of the highest-earning crisps salesmen in the world, onto that old familiar pitch he looks up at the steep empty terraces around him with a hint of nostalgia in his eyes and says something about the bits of paper, the famous ticker-tape, and about how Argentina is the only place in the world where that happens. Lineker asks whether it's bothersome, playing with all that paper snow flying around in one's face and Kempes just tuts, still looking up into the past, back to a moment when he tasted happiness.

That happiness was not unique to him. Many, many people are very grateful to those young men of '78, very happy to have been allowed that month of joy in the middle of hell. Menotti protected the players from the talk outside their training ground and kept the media happy with his articulate philosophy of football. The nation concentrated on the game and the players became national heroes.

But societies can be unkind to their heroes: of the twenty-two young men from that 1978 Argentine squad few have truly remained established in the mainstream of the football business. Menotti, of course, their chain-smoking intellectual left-wing manager, is still in the world's premier league. Indeed, while Lineker is in Argentina Menotti leaves Independiente for Sampdoria in a surprise mid-season move which means he cancels his interview with Gary Lineker. Work first. Daniel Passarella, captain of the '78 side, is now national coach. But whereas his career has not let him down, his son died in a tragic accident two years ago. Goalkeeper Fillol also has known twentieth-century disorders – his daughter is a very severe anorexic. Tarantini, still regarded around the world as a defender of some excellence, fell into the world of drugs and rock 'n' roll. He too was imprisoned on account of the young girls and judges saga relating to Coppola, eventually released because he's an E-addict, not a peddler. Tarantini cuts a tragic figure now; he could be seen sitting as a stage ornament on a sofa at the America TV studios the day Maradona started his own show. Rene Houseman, a frail-looking old man who wanders round the pool bars of his neighbourhood on lazy afternoons. Ricky Villa – the man who scored the historic goal at Wembley – recently sacked as manager of second division club Quilmes. The individual histories of those young men are the recent history of Argentina. Heroes under an enemy government, for twenty years now they have lived with the burden of having to justify the fact that they went onto the pitch and gave their best. They have to apologise for having tried so hard, for having succeeded. Heroes twenty years ago, now members of that other club: the ex-footballers without a decent pension.

The day after Lineker's visit to Rosario, he goes to interview Passarella, who is holding a press conference before a World Cup qualifier against Peru. At the training ground near Ezeiza airport – the same ground used during 1978, just opposite the military school – hundreds of journalists gather round Lineker, cluttering his path by shoving mikes and recorders under his nose. The crowd around him starts growing, in the way crowds do. Eventually all that can be seen is an enormous scrum, Lineker standing politely in the middle, unable to walk in any direction because he is totally surrounded, answering every question in his perfect Spanish, rewarding individual journalists with a special delivery of his dreamy eyes and friendly smile. When Passarella starts talking in the press room there are more people outside huddled around Lineker than inside listening to the wisdoms of the man in charge of the national team. Even one of the players from the current squad goes up to Lineker to express admiration – he was a kid in 1986, watching the games on the telly, and has admired Lineker ever since. 'It was close. You could have given us some trouble,' he says, in awe still.

This kind of thing will happen again and again. The men of the River Plate have Lineker so clearly registered in their minds that one time, when filming a typical barbecue in a market, Lineker sits down to eat his meal and the two men sitting at the counter besides him clock him instantly without even looking up from their plates. 'He's got a Greek profile,' one of them says to the other, hinting with the slightest movement of his head that he means Lineker. He pauses briefly and adds, again without looking up: 'He wasn't the greatest player you've ever seen, but he always had the goal right here,' and to emphasise the last two words he lifts his index finger to the little dent between his eyebrows, *entre ceja y ceja* (Spanish for 'between brow and brow'). And both men carry on eating their steaks, quite satisfied with their observation.

'A good goalscorer has to be a little bit like a thief,' Passarella tells Lineker. 'All defenders think like thieves,' Lineker will remark later. 'They have to.' It's an unfortunate metaphor which removes all the fantasy of playful elegance and suggests instead that it is the code for survival of the back streets that's carried onto the pitch. Passarella is teaching young men to steal, and Lineker is sticking up for him. But in fact, Lineker is not partisan either way. He can make sense out of things, he can interpret, but it is only because he is such a natural diplomat that he instinctively strives to couch 'what was said' by the other into something coherent and pragmatic. Lineker probably couldn't care less whether or not Passarella is a thief, a hero, an arsehole or what. He just behaves like a gentleman, no matter what the situation.

Gary Lineker is a very contained man. He has made a career out of an image, both of which are very important to him. He is Gary Lineker twenty-four hours a day, and is never rude, or moody, or aggressive. He has a quick grasp of the rules at play in any given situation and adjusts to them. He is, after all, a man who has never been booked. This is what Argentinians find most remarkable – an outstanding career in international professional football without a single yellow card – together with his Spanish.

It is not the norm for English visitors to Patagonia to speak fluent Spanish. But after winning the Golden Boot in 1986 he was signed up by Barcelona (or maybe it was before, maybe knowing that contract was being negotiated played a part in encouraging all those goals. Maybe some goalscorers are more like business-men than thieves.) and moved with his wife, Michelle, to one of the grooviest, most happening cities in Europe. Playing for a club that is more an institution than perhaps any other club in the world, on a weekly wage that was already 'considerably more' than that commanded by some of the current top-paid Premier League stars, Golden Boot winner and national hero back home, fair play awards to boot, Mr Lineker would lie awake at night, staring at the ceiling and going over the Spanish learnt that day. He would make himself learn it, by sheer force of will power. Maybe he did that with football – maybe he would lie in bed going over moves, reliving shots at goal, mentally turning his thigh half an inch and trying again.

His concentration is still unique: 'Do everything as well as possible, with the minimum effort necessary,' he imparts. And it sounds like the secret formula for a stress-free life: in the van, Lineker can re-write links and questions in minutes. At a shoot, he can switch his performance for the camera in seconds and become 'the BBC interviewer' with ease. He can be 'one of the team', cracking jokes on the back row, or a European with the presence of a bigwig exec on the golf course. He switches on, concentrates on the immediate issue, performs, delivers. But he doesn't fret, and he doesn't look like he's trying hard, and he has the air of one who is not 'taking his work home with him'. Yet at night, when he can't sleep, he can think hard and improve himself. As a result he is able to grasp all the nuances of conversational Spanish, to a degree unusual for someone who has learnt a language as an adult.

Yet in his chosen trade, Mr Lineker is not supposed to be cognitively unusual or outstandingly mathematical in his conceptual representation of the world. He is there to fix his soft brown eyes on the camera, do his to-die-for smile, look like he would feel bad if he accidentally trod on an ant, and keep selling those crisps. Or deliver lines in that millennium version of the panto, *They Think It's All Over*. Or travel the world 'in search of his goal-scoring roots' (his own words). In the mostly mediocre world in which he currently makes his living, his higher-order cognitive skills come well after his image, and the lack of stains on that limits the potential for gossip or lively debate. It's not hard to find unkind comments made about anyone, but *industry* rumours about *Gary* don't get any nastier than: 'Gary's OK as long as you feed him the lines', 'Gary doesn't really get enthusiastic about anything', 'Let's hope Gary isn't too bland', 'Gary's not up to politics/culture/society/anything but game-of-two-halves-speak'. These are unfair. But Gary Lineker doesn't know this. Not that such things are said about him, he knows that. He doesn't know they are unfair. In reality he houses a curious mind where endless relevant questions and pertinent quips are entertained.

'Why isn't there a different word for "the" when it's used to mean "the one and only"?' Gary asks thoughtfully, from out of nowhere, one time. 'Like when you say *The* Ten, meaning Maradona, "the" means something different to when you say the sugar. For example: *the* night, *the* game, *the* goal. The "one and only the" is a different "the" to the more general "thes"; when "the" means just one of something. There should be a different word for it.' He has inadvertently triggered off a philosophical conversation and someone suggests that this is in fact one of the most interesting questions of modern philosophy. The issue was addressed most extensively by Bertrand Russell in his *Theory of Definite Descriptions*. It has been the focus of attention of some of the most important philosophers of meaning but there is really no definitive explanation of why this is so. 'Is it really one of the main questions of philosophy?' Lineker looks genuinely chuffed.

Philosophical ponderings aside, it is certainly the case that Mr Lineker is more than up to the challenges posed by his current activities. Trapped by English society's desire to think of footballers as 'stupid' and by the anti-intellectual mood that prevails in English culture, he most probably will never pursue his more abstract powers of thought. This isn't to say he will not continue to prosper as a mezzo-brow figure in contemporary football culture. Although there is money to be made in the crisps industry, Lineker is keen to preserve his status as a clever man of football; he made his move into 'journalism' with the same refined sense of opportunity and timing with which he scored all those magnificent goals. He wrote a 'learning' column for the *Observer* which served him as the stepping stone into the BBC. He could have gone for a tabloid and commanded a considerably higher fee from the start, but he knew – as did Jon

Holmes – that the BBC would never take him seriously if he did that. Now he's well on his way to becoming the next Des Lynam. And that's exactly how he wants it.

He is known as Mr Nice, often described as 'too good to be true' and more unkindly as 'a jellyfish with no sting' but he is also, bizarrely, middle-England's middle-of-the-road frustrated housewife's dream pin-up-boy, a charmer one could definitely introduce to one's mother. He was launched into this particular aspect of his marketable attributes after the 1990 World Cup, when he inspired the play *An Evening With Gary Lineker*, so named because that is the ultimate dream of the jealous wife of a football-obsessed En-Ger-land supporter. But as well as being this one-dimensional TV talking head, he's a clever bloke who can do his best when he needs to. And his best is good.

Such people are entitled to indulge themselves now and again, to seek a little treat for themselves. So it's surprising to hear that when Mr Lineker expresses the desire to travel with his golf clubs, people consider him flamboyant and difficult. Still, he travels with them anyway, and good thing too because this means he can go and let off steam at the shooting range mid-week. It's all very well being Mr Nice in Spanish, mobbed by a people for whom football is most definitely more than just a game, or just a job, or just entertainment and for whom, within football, Lineker is more than just a 'Golden Boot'. It's all very well assimilating a new culture, speaking highly of Maradona publicly, honouring the game of football by never having been booked, and working around the sensitivities of a nation which, let's face it, won a World Cup with a handball. Mr Nice will perform and he will not let the side down. But there must be some moment of the day, some time when he wishes he could just say 'fuck off' to someone, when he'd rather behave like a spoilt celebrity, be rude, or just say, 'Look, I don't really care. In my case it could have been cricket.' And that's why it's important to allow him to travel with his golf clubs, and ensure golf is always a possible option when there's a couple of hours to kill.

Such an opportunity arises after Passarella and the other interviews of the day are over, and just before the filming schedule demands a visit to a tango bar. The deal is he won't be made to dance but he knows he will be set up and he knows, also, that he will do it. Dancing tango is probably only just on the right side of the line which marks Gary's 'no-go area'. Wearing a tutu for Walker's crisps, for example, has stayed on the wrong side. Never mind how much money we're talking about. The *Golden Boots* series is not really money motivated, it's more of a conceptual thing, but Gary's got a cut of international sales ('That's where the money is. Why do you think I'm doing this?'). So, to a large extent, he will go through the motions, and while he does not believe tango has anything to do with football, really, he appreciates that BBC prime-time viewers might want a token 'travelogue' gesture. He will dance tango, and he will deliver 'the lines fed', and he will do it all with a smile.

And in actual fact he endures more than that. The sleazy atmosphere of the tango bar and the sensual low lighting encourage some of his troupe to drink a little bit too much and behave a little bit obtrusively while the show is on. A few people hiss for silence as a drunken team-mate from the En-Ger-Lish clan falls squarely onto a chair at some complete strangers' table. Lineker is horrified to hear the culprit slur: 'It's OK, I'm with Gary Lineker.' The reputation of the English abroad is one of Lineker's main intellectual preoccupations. He blushes but keeps his composure. He might have been less prone to if he hadn't been able to wander off to the driving range a little earlier. For a wee break.

He had settled down in his booth with a basket containing several hundred little white balls. The driving range is by the riverfront, and at dusk the end of the range and the beginning of the sky merge into one single expanse of dark. With his knees slightly bent, muscles tense, a vein in his thick neck bulging, eyes fixed firmly on the ball, then raised to an invisible target in the distance, then back on the ball, Gary Lineker grasped the golf club and breathed like a professional. A little bounce on the spot, a couple of swings that stop short of the ball, another look at the horizon, somewhere beyond the darkness, and whack! He loosened up again and delivered his familiar smile loaded with relief. Even his eyebrows seemed to lose some of that protruding Greekness after each shot.

It's a funny thing golf, because it requires total concentration for very brief spurts of time. Total concentration, and complete motor-visual skills. It looks a bit boring on telly, but it actually requires more muscles all over the body to be positioned just so, more control of strength and speed than most other games. When this mental and physical duet is not called for, business matters may be attended to. Men love golf. Football men love golf. Ossie Ardiles was sacked as manager of Spurs, but the day after he was on the golf course before dawn. President Menem of Argentina, who is not very good at golf, says: 'If you just strike one ball well, you stay in a good mood for the rest of the day.' It's hard to imagine that someone might achieve so much success and power in life that a good mood becomes a precious commodity. But for a substantial amount of people for whom this is so, golf beats therapy anytime.

At the driving range the man in the booth adjacent to Lineker's turns round. He points an accusatory finger at Lineker: he's recognised him. He immediately invites the celebrity to play golf at Buenos Aires' most exclusive club at the weekend. Sorry, I'm working, volunteers Mr Nice without a hint of irritation, despite the man's forceful insistence.

As it turns out, Gary will play golf at that very club over the weekend. With the president of Argentina. And he will be working.

★　★　★

President Menem is a Peronist leader who is about as close to Peronism as Tony Blair is to Old Labour. Peron was a larger-than-life Argentine leader, a true populist who on Sunday afternoons would walk from the government house to his club, Boca Juniors. When his Ambassador to Moscow met Stalin, Stalin's first question was 'And how are Boca Juniors performing this year?' Books have been written looking at the relationship of various Argentine presidents to sport and Mr Menem's chapter is certainly a colourful one. Once a racing driver, he loves sport much more than politics, and he loves politics. He reinstated Argentina's Grand Prix, vehemently backed a campaign to host the 2004 Olympics, and appointed top-flight sports stars to his cabinet. He himself is a sportsman who supports River Plate, Boca's arch-rivals. He doesn't go to games anymore because he can't be seen swearing, he says. There was a time when Menem was considered a jinx, and he didn't go to games because of that. But he regularly hosts TV viewing sessions at his residence in the neighbourhood of Olivos, where Maradona and Coppola are frequent guests.

An interview with Menem has been agreed but finalising the details proves to be a task and a half. Menem has heard that Lineker is a keen golfer and they will play golf together, but for security reasons specifics about where and at what time cannot be given over the telephone. Perhaps Lineker will go to the presidential residence and then fly in the presidential helicopter to a golf club. But then how will the crew and cameras get there? After at least one hundred phone calls it is finally established that Lineker will go to the presidential palace where he will meet the president. Then they will drive together to the golf club where the crew will be waiting. One hundred phone calls.

As it is planned, so it is carried out. At the Olivos residence Mr Lineker is introduced to President Menem and to Mr

Constancio Vigil, owner and director of a local publishing house which has among its titles *El Grafico*, Latin America's best-known football magazine. Vigil is to be Lineker's golf partner. Over coffee served on a silver tray the terrible problems of football violence are discussed politely, if somewhat hurriedly; this chat is not what any of these men are interested in. They gulp their coffee down and jump up excitedly when one of the presidential aides says the cars are ready.

The golfing party is split among three identical burgundy cars. The presidential residence is in fact almost a small village, with roads and security within as well as hefty gates leading to the outside. It has become known as the Olivos 'multisports complex'. The three cars move as one as they turn into the street to take the highway. There is no police escort, no obvious security to be seen. The cars never allow a gap of more than twenty metres or so to come between them and they drive at high speed, in radio contact with each other and presumably a helicopter overhead. The toll gates open up mysteriously just before the cars are due to hit them. The three burgundy cars speed comfortably along the motorway out of Buenos Aires city, past endless kilometres of rubbish dumps and shanty towns which paint a folkloric if disturbing picture of third world reality. Then, again as one, the three vehicles turn off the motorway onto a long, winding road set in a wild forest. Immersed in the hilly, windy, Pampean backdrop is a chalet straight out of a Bond movie, complete with floor-to-ceiling windows on every corner to maximise the view. This is the Golf Club.

Formalities are dealt with first, so as to be able to truly relax while they play – this is the president's preference. And Messrs Menem and Lineker are miked up. In TV terms, the interview is a success. Lineker is at his best, Menem relaxed and frank. He tells of how he watched the 1978 World Cup in prison. 'Would you rather have been a footballer than a president?' asks

Lineker. 'Of course,' says Menem emphatically. Then Gary says something about how difficult it has proved to reach Maradona and Menem looks mildly puzzled, says it's unusual for a president to intervene in matters such as this but, as he looks up to one of his aides, where is Maradona anyway and can they call him right now? Maradona is interned in Villa La Angostura, in the south of Argentina, planning to return to Buenos Aires the next day. If he can see you, Menem tells Lineker, you will get to visit one of the most beautiful places in the world.

Coppola's reaction upon being contacted via Menem will have to be defined by imagination. What he does know is that Gary Lineker is in town making a documentary because it has been put to him via American TV that a meeting between Maradona and Lineker in front of a camera would not be an altogether bad TV idea. Imagine:

Diego Maradona, the genius who would blow a million-dollar meeting out for a quick screw any day if he felt like it, the rebel from the slums who still travels without a tie, the archetypal hero from the millennium fairy tale who walks straight past Havelange at World Cups without shaking his hand, never afraid to speak his *feelings* let alone his mind, the crazy little giant who dices with death and toboggans into hell on a daily basis because *any* compromise is just too painful . . . MEETS . . . Gary Lineker, the clean-cut gentleman who stoops to conquer the natives, the white middle-class family man who is proud of his business, the restrained TV professional who won the Golden Boot because he rose above himself one day on a football pitch; rose above himself and the situation and overcame both the anger at a goal against England clearly handled into the net and the astonishment at the sight of that same little devil dribbling past only a few yards away with what has become regarded by some as 'the only miracle of the twentieth century' (and that was a Dutchman who said that) and by Lineker as a goal he wanted 'to cheer, right there on the pitch – I've never seen anything like it'.

Imagine that. Showing at a television screen in your home. That's Box Office.

'Stop, stop, you're making the hairs on the back of my neck stand on end!' shouts a local average football supporter, ABC-1, Maradona-loving and Lineker-respecting young man when he hears the idea. And even though Argentina boasts two Golden Boot winners and Maradona is not one of them, the series is also interested.

Coppola has been approached, therefore, already. But Maradona doesn't like to do anything predictable and a reply of any sort would have been predictable. Time is running out for the Lineker clan, driving around the Pampas in a van, stopping now and again to shoot images of relevance to the goalscorers or attempting to add local flavour with images of the port at sunset, the barbecues, or the sleazy tango bars. Menem's offer to intervene is not to be snubbed, and although hiring a private jet to visit Maradona in the south is logistically and financially totally out of the question, it suddenly seems that maybe the meeting might become a reality. The president has elevated the concept to an entirely new level.

The interview is followed by a presidential–celebrity golf round, followed by a private lunch. 'Who won?' someone asks. Menem says, 'They did.' Constancio Vigil, Lineker's partner, makes some mumbling noises to indicate that the win ought to be disallowed because of something or other but Menem shakes his head discreetly. 'He won,' he mouths pointing at Lineker. What apparently happened was that they were on the green of the last hole, Menem to putt, when a mobile phone rang and Menem missed the hole. Then Lineker's partner said to Lineker that perhaps he should miss, they should let Menem win, because the phone had gone off and that. And Lineker bent his knees, flexed his muscles, tensed his neck, looked at the ball, then at the hole, then at the ball again, maybe at the president, and whissh! Stroked the ball straight into the hole. Because above everything, he is a professional sportsman.

It is almost as if Menem likes the fact that Lineker didn't let him win. He respects him more. Even though he's lost the game he's in a very good mood over lunch, cracking jokes round the table. The owner of the club joins his VIP guests for a few moments and recommends that Menem have his own golf course built. 'The hell I've had to endure over a small landing strip for my plane,' says Menem alluding to one of the most notorious allegations of corruption his administration has come under. 'All I need is to build my own golf club!' and he laughs heartily. You won't be president forever, imagine how nice it would be then to . . . but Menem interrupts such misplaced comfort. *'Nobody* will let me win when I'm not the president,' he says with a tinge of sadness.

They are to return to town by private plane, and Lineker, who is afraid of flying, pulls a face. 'Mr Lineker has a fear of flying, Mr President' someone says, and Menem, whose own son died in a helicopter crash, says he can go in the car then, thinking maybe he doesn't have a penis after all, this English Lineker. But Lineker's pride has been dented and he says what nonsense, of course he isn't afraid. So the golfing party proceeds to the presidential private jet for a spectacular low flight over the province of Buenos Aires, in the true James Bond style that befits the occasion.

Lineker believes that Eric Cantona kung-fu kicking that xenophobe was *wrong*. He cannot find that kind of behaviour justifiable on any grounds, his mind has no way of conceiving a scenario in which Cantona's action might be described as the heroic act of a young poet driven by an endless pursuit of justice. Lineker is not intellectually limited in any way, but his suspension of disbelief will not cross certain domains. His interlocutor's insistence that one could argue that although what Cantona did was wrong he did it for the right reasons, exasperates him. 'You just don't do that! Unless you're a nutter!' he shouts indignantly. It's so rare to see Lineker expressing himself so vehemently, he seems genuinely angry: a football player hitting a supporter is totally not on. No. N.O.

Lineker is a public figure and he takes this fact seriously. It's not that he lets it go to his head – quite the contrary. 'I'm a back row boy, I'm one of the team,' he insists. 'Always have been, always will be.' With his co-workers he is team-spirited, good-humoured, and light-hearted. But he understands the responsibilities and the shag about this whole 'celebrity' stuff. He knows if a crowd of children run into him in the street he will have to spend some time signing autographs, and he has learnt to spot them coming early and walk the other way decisively and fast, but with a minimum of fuss. Being a celebrity is a full-time occupation and celebrities shouldn't ever let their guard down. Never. Wherever they are, even in their most private and intimate moments – particularly in their most private and intimate moments – the publicness of their very being could turn into their worst nightmare if they don't watch out. That the extravagant and impulsive behaviour of the likes of Eric Cantona and Diego Maradona has more than once backfired on them is undisputable, but to Gary Lineker there are certain things that are simply unimaginable.

Playing for England was a job. A really good job which paid well and allowed him one of his favourite satisfactions which is goalscoring. The job involved certain social responsibilities such as dealing with the press now and again, trying to not get off your head and piss in a glass at a Buckingham Palace garden party if you ever happened to find yourself there, and generally give En-Ger-Land the impression that you were out there trying to make it happen for them. As contractual obligations, the job required a certain amount of rather tedious training and the commitment to spend ninety minutes exerting every neuron, nerve and cell in your mind/body in pursuit of a result.

Lineker delivered the results, and more. He was good at his job; in fact, he was outstanding. He did as well as a player can. And he was such an accomplished all-rounder in the business of business, in the understanding of football as the industry within which he worked, that just before his playing years were about to come to their natural devaluation he found himself in the enviable position of being able to make a choice. 'For a while I thought I'd like to become involved in the running of the game, make things better,' he confesses. And he says it with a hint of melancholy, like Robbie Robertson when he says he wrote *The Night They Drove Old Dixie Down* when 'we thought we could change the world – now we know all we can do is help the neighbourhood'.

But unlike Cantona or Maradona, Gary Lineker isn't under the delusion that he was put on this earth as some kind of messiah, he doesn't feel he's on a personal crusade to eliminate evil from the football establishment. He's a salesman, not a revolutionary or a politician (although he would make a good politician). He also doesn't have profound existential problems about football, and what it represents. When asked what happened on the bus after England got knocked out in Italy, what did they all do, what did they say to *Waddle*? He states matter of factly: 'You just take the mickey, try to have a laff. You've got to, haven't ya?' And when he tries to establish what it is that makes football such a different thing in Argentina to what it is in England, for example, he concludes that maybe in England 'we know it doesn't matter that much.'

Cut to: Maradona's press conference in USA '94 when he's expelled from the finals due to traces of ephedrine found in his urine. A man broken; psychologically, morally, physically: 'I don't mean to over-dramatise but believe me, they've chopped my legs off. *They've taken us out of the World Cup and they've taken us out of the illusion*' is what he said, 'and above everything I think they've taken me out of football forever.'

In Gary Lineker's case, retirement from playing football was triggered by a mysterious foot injury. He retired once and once only and has never kicked a ball again since. He says it's because of his foot but it's possible that, like Pelé, he is determined not to dent the memory of better days by perhaps not being able to do it anymore. And he got on with his life, and with his work, no longer a football player. Managing was totally out of the question. You still have to go to training, but you're not allowed to score the goals anymore. And Lineker likes feeling he's 'one of the team'. He doesn't rate the dynamic between manager and players, he doesn't think he would have enjoyed that job. The Walkers deal probably means he need never work again if he doesn't want to, but he will. Because he is not the rock 'n' roller type who can sit around, he doesn't do drugs – really, never – and he's too restless. He would get bored if he didn't work. 'Journalism' seemed like a good avenue to pursue. Journalism, and marketing his own image of course.

And he also finds himself sitting in a radio commentary booth at the Monumental stadium in Argentina, airing informed opinions on a second-rate game which is being played against Peru. The game is transmitted live in Uruguayan Victor Hugo Morales' show, and Lineker's being filmed for the Beeb while Victor Hugo delivers his legendary commentaries and eternal shouts of 'GOOOOOOOL'. When he's not commentating on a live game, Victor Hugo combines tango and poetry with football.

He says football is a form of expression based, as is art, on 'harmony, symmetry, geometry'. He refers to Lineker as a 'gentleman' on air ('How can you never have fouled?' someone asks Lineker. 'Not never have fouled. Never been booked!' he replied, almost offended at the accusation) and has promised his son that if they ever visit England he will endeavour to introduce him to the only player in the world who has never been shown a yellow card. 'It can also be seen as a business,' Victor Hugo will sometimes concede about football.

Earlier that day Lineker has played golf with an Australian TV exec who has spent the last two years hopping from various Hyatt and Hilton hotels into chauffeur-driven limos. He has done this in every major city in Latin America, and although he doesn't know much about football he knows all he needs to: 'You're simply not in the market if you haven't got soccer down here,' he pronounces. Because it is a special tourist attraction, he will go to the game. He is alone and, unbelievably, in the middle of the hectic live transmission, Lineker manages to start a Chinese whisper in order to ensure someone sees the Australian safely back to his chauffeur-driven car.

And while Gary Lineker and Victor Hugo commentate on the match live on Argentine radio and the BBC records the event for UK broadcast later, mobile phones galore are ringing outside the little cabin. The heat is on from Maradona's people who, instigated by Menem's people, are approaching Lineker's people to sort out this Box Office dream of an encounter. And Mauro Viale's people are calling too. The heat is on.

It's 2.00 a.m. in Buenos Aires and Gary Lineker's phone rings. Guillermo Coppola is on the line, suggesting they do the interview then. Can't Gary come over now? Gary Lineker in his best Spanish explains that he is already in bed: 'I'm English, you see.' He agrees to attend Maradona's press conference about his return to football the following day.

It's hard to know whether or not, if Lineker had woken up the crew and made his way to the Olivos multisports-centre, he would have got an interview. A local journalist later says: 'He missed out on the story of his life! He said "I'm English" and missed out!' He most certainly missed out on the *night* of his life; but to a clean-cut Englishman who walks out of nightclubs completely sober at 3.00 a.m. it might have presented an uncomfortable situation. Maybe he missed out on something good, maybe he missed out on something bad. Like the tutu, there are certain things Gary Lineker will not do.

But he does attend the press conference the next day, and again has an opportunity to reflect on the social meaning of the slums which adorn the country's highways on the way there. He crosses the suspension bridge over the mouth (literally, La Boca) of the River Plate. It is on the muddy shores of La Boca that football first arrived in the country, over a hundred years ago. The colours of the winter sun taint the shabby corrugated iron houses with a certain beauty. Just outside a large shanty town, practically on the motorway itself, a football game is being played. An enormous crowd has gathered to watch. 'For me that scene sums up everything I've seen about football in Argentina,' says Lineker almost to himself for in the van the crew are asleep again.

Maradona's press conference is being held at a Red Cross Centre in the city of La Plata. Hectic preparations are underway for the arrival of The Ten, and Lineker poses for photographs with Red Cross volunteers. He says he does 'a lot of work with the Red Cross in England'. Maradona, who we know by now has had a late night, is very late in arriving. The football match is scheduled to begin live on America TV: Maradona's people keep calling in with travel updates. 'We're near the airport', 'we're getting into the plane', 'we'll be flying out of town shortly'. The little Red Cross soldiers who are waiting in perfect formation for Maradona's arrival begin to get tired and restless, and the people crammed in the modest back room where drinks and snacks have been carefully laid out on paper table-cloths are becoming slightly tetchy as the hours go by. Gary Lineker is among them, clutching some Argentina shirts for Maradona to sign, but cheerfully doing most of the signing himself.

When Maradona finally arrives, he comes and goes like a little hurricane among the crowd. Suddenly everyone is converged in a giant scrum, like flies around honey or seagulls around a trawler, they hover around an invisible being that is breaking his way round the tables from inside the buzz. Hidden behind his absurd shades, wearing an equally absurd baseball cap, pushing his chest forward and his shoulders slightly back, Maradona walks in and out of that room weaving his miniature self through the mob with the skill of the man who scored that second goal in Mexico. Part of the way he does this is by *not looking at anybody*, a weird way he has of elevating himself above his own body and registering panoramic views of the terrain he will have to cross. When he's like this, he doesn't do autographs or any of that celebrity interactive stuff. Least of all is he likely to respond to interview requests.

Gary Lineker does not take his role as a journalist so much to heart that he will behave like a seagull following a trawler in the hope that some crumbs will break off. He stands far from the buzz observing the scene with some detachment and when Maradona leaves for the stadium and Coppola says to Lineker 'come with us, we can do it in the dressing room', Lineker responds like a classical number ten, thinks, pauses for a moment and delivers. He says, 'No.'

the rage of giggs

JOE BOYLE

. . . a new sound behind me, no longer muddy or gravelly. Goose bumps I never knew I possessed – on the soles of my feet, across my eyeballs – spring erect. Curious when written, curious when spoken, mellifluous when sung by a choir of Tenor-Gods like the ones behind me, is the Welsh language. The conductor has his body turned from the band to the crowd and is listening to them, conducting them, appreciating them.

This is the World Cup.

12.28 p.m., Wednesday 11 December 1996: The M4 between Cardiff and Newport, South Wales

We're late, the 'Meet the Players Session' is starting and we're still several miles off. Phil Suarez, my driver, is telling me that press conferences with Bobby Gould, the Welsh national team coach, are usually insane affairs. Apparently, 'Mrs Gould's had a bad week' is a frequent introduction. Boasting about how it took him just three hours to drive back from covering Cardiff at Hartlepool last season, Phil hurls the car into a reserved hotel parking space. Wobbling, I take my first look at the Stakis Hotel and know that Wales are going out of the World Cup.

If you want to know how a national team is going to perform, ignore what the coaches, players and players' wives say; disregard form and tradition; pooh-pooh soothsayers, cranks and journalists. Concentrate, instead, on hotel janitors.

During Euro 96, I took advantage of being in the vicinity of the Bulgarian squad and, following them on their dyspeptic campaign, became convinced that the way a team plays reflects the aura of their hotel. Ill at ease, the Bulgarians moved three times in five days before ending up in what seemed like a breeze-block prison to the north of Newcastle. None of the other guests seemed to know, or care, who they were and half the squad didn't seem to know, or care, who the other half were. The odd exception aside, they were untalkative and unsmiling. That was before Stoichkov padded in, at which point the rest looked really miserable.

Sure enough, when it came to the football the three good Bulgarians – Balakov, Letchkov and Stoichkov – passed the ball to each other and nobody else. In front of half-empty stadiums, they bickered and sulked before sloping back to the hotel. Where, having hogged the ball all day, Letchkov and Balakov proceeded to hog the pool table.

There is therefore no doubt that if the Brazilians of 1970 had ever had to prepare for a match at the Stakis Hotel, Newport, they would have lost, no matter who the opposition. Even the Welsh side of 1997-98.

If the Welsh management had hoped to prepare for their crucial World Cup qualifying match against Turkey in peaceful solitude, something had gone wrong. The foyer was swarming with hundreds of greying women, sipping sherry and grimacing while a tuneless school choir sang tuneless Christmas carols.

As it happened, Phil – part-time financial adviser, part-time footie correspondent for Red Dragon FM – could have taken his time: the session had in fact started at 12.00, not 12.30 as most of the media had been told. As all but a few had missed the conference it was extended into the players' lunch. 'Let's hope this is the bad luck out of the way,' BBC Wales' interviewer was saying to Gould. Gould smiled weakly. He knew something the rest of us knew.

It was a curious event, this combination of player interviews and players' lunch. The food looked disgusting but paid lip service to current trends: rubber chicken breast, even rubberier pasta, cannelloni and what looked like tinned mixed rubber. The name players were being interviewed, the rest eating, the established squad members in cheery groups. In contrast were the younger, newer players, grim and chewing, chewing, chewing in miserable isolation. They left early.

Vinnie Jones was strolling around in shorts, socks rolled to his ankles. Carrying a full plate of food, he walked about the room striking other players on the back of the neck with it, laughing like a schoolboy. His victims ignored him. Like tinned veg, Jones is an acquired taste. He ambled up to Phil and, with a whoop, thrust the plate in his face. 'Fuck off Jones,' said Suarez. 'I'm a vegetarian.'

'Simplicity is genius,' I overheard Gould saying as I approached Barry Horne, all winning smile and fluency. Horne admitted that he knew absolutely nothing about the Turkish players but didn't think that such a bad idea. Five yards away, Dean Saunders, another pleasant man, was talking about how he hoped to share his knowledge of the Turks gained during a recent, unsuccessful spell playing for Galatasaray. Saunders, who had not been scoring for Nottingham Forest, was constantly interrupted by a stream of piss-taking from a group on a nearby table, its ringleader Neville Southall, Gould's second-in-command and leader on the pitch. With each jibe at his current lean form, Saunders would smile (just), pause and continue his analysis.

Suddenly the man from the *South Wales Echo* came running up, glee in his face, to drag us to an adjoining room. Rows of seats had been arranged in front of a screen that covered most of the far wall. A video was playing and it took a few moments to register what was being shown. Then an orange, Dutch shirt, a flash of blond hair – Bergkamp – a smear of ball, boof! Goal! Southall sprawling, a new angle, blond hair, boof! Goal! Southall stationary, Bowen and Symons colliding, a blond boof! Angle, Goal! Orange, Orange, Orange, Boof! Boof! Boof! Now van Hooijdonk's crew cut, a bloated net, boof! Defenders departed, Southall hands on hips. BOOF! BOOF! BOOF! (Or 'SGORIO! SGORIO! SGORIO!' as they say in Welsh.)

For ten minutes we watched a masterful display of TV editing as the ten goals the Welsh had conceded to the Dutch in their previous two qualifying games were shown from every conceivable angle and then some. With each viewing the gaps got bigger, the marking slacker, the stumbling more hilarious. And to cap it all was the accompanying sound-track: Queen's 'I Am the Invisible Man'. Standing inches from the screen, in the eye of the storm, was Gould, hand on chin, upper body angled slightly towards the screen, his magnificent, startling eye-brows drawn together, trying to absorb a message, a meaning, inspiration while the ball just kept hitting the back of the net. Boof! The Welsh defenders were as absent from the room as they had been on the pitch.

I found one, Andy Melville, moping around the foyer where the women had sat down to lunch. His attempts to escape Gould's psychology lesson were being foiled by the booming bass of the music which continued to bounce down the corridor. Melville was a hapless defender in Welsh colours despite having a good season with Sunderland (my team), who were playing less than twenty-four hours after the Turkey match.

'Who's going to replace you?' I blurted. 'Bally?' The total inappropriateness of this cryptic question, its unexpectedness, not to mention its abysmal execution deeply confused Melville. 'No,' he squeaked, not knowing what I was banging on about.

He was looking truly miserable: none of the press had asked him a question all day and then some loony . . . He wandered off for treatment on his groin strain.

This was the World Cup.

3.00 p.m., Thursday 12 December 1996: Cardiff Arms Park

The Cardiff Arms Park is a fantastic sports venue, admirable for being slap bang in the centre of the city. Having said which, it was clear on arriving for the training session that the grass was much too long for football; the Welsh rugby team were playing a friendly against Australia less than twenty-four hours after this crucial game.

There was a buzz in the stadium, provided mainly by a large number of primary school children who'd been allowed in to watch the session. Their excitement wasn't infectious and the players lolled around, a few of them involved in a desultory round of 'keepy-uppy'. In time a practice game was arranged, the Under-21s against a half-strength full squad. The big guns – Ryan Giggs and Mark Hughes included – were held back to do a few sprinting exercises. Giggs came last each time. Nothing to prove.

After fifteen minutes, the sprinting stars were dragged into action. Giggs, tight on the wing, looked terminally bored and his first touch of the game was abysmal. On several occasions in the opening minutes he lost the ball, and spent most of the time crimping his curls. Needing to prove his fitness, Hughes' first two touches were equally terrible. He kicked the ground in frustration, snarled and charged after a teenage defender. Suddenly, for the first time, there was an edge. And then Giggs threw a sublime dummy that had everyone double-taking.

A few rows behind me sat the unpicked Vinnie Jones, talking 'fucking' conspiratorially with a 'fucking' group of 'fucking' officials. I strained to listen and concluded that his brief, uninspiring international career was drawing to an end. His coterie was feeding him lines. 'How do you cook pheasant, Vinnie?' one asked. 'Just turn the fucking oven on,' he replied. Ha, ha, ha, ha, ha, ha, ha, ha, ha.

Jones got his turn half an hour later in a two-touch kick-around. The first player to be chosen, he turned to his conspirators on the touchline. 'Boys know the story,' he gloated. 'First fucking picked.' That might have been the case, but he was the last ever passed to. He charged around, impressive and enthusiastic, taking up good positions, but rarely received the ball.

Finally, shooting practice. Two thrilled young boys were dispatched behind the goal to fetch loose balls and started energetically, chasing everything. But so shoddy was the shooting that after ten minutes they had ground to a halt and were slumped against a wall, knackered and breathless. By the time the header and volleys session had produced a final strike rate of about 3 per cent the stadium had gone very quiet.

As the players walked off, I asked John Hartson if it had been a successful session. He grinned. I approached Andy Melville again. Fear flickered across his eyes on seeing me, but my question was better delivered and he monosyllabled me an answer. Bringing up the rear was Gould. 'No interviews,' he pre-empted me. 'A successful session?' I persevered. He turned away as he answered and I misheard him. It could have been 'No interviews' again. It could have been 'No.' I walked with Vinnie Jones to the bus and asked him what the difference was between playing at international and domestic level. 'It's different,' he replied. 'After all, you're living with a group of players for a whole week.' Enough searching questions.

Leaving, I spotted a nattily dressed man, clearly a Turk, who had infiltrated the session. We talked.

'So Mehmet,' I asked. 'Have you seen anything today to frighten the Turkish team?'

'No.'

5.00 p.m., Saturday 14 December 1996: A store room, Cardiff Arms Park

Actually, neither team did enough to frighten the other. 0-0. In isolation, not necessarily a terrible result. In context, the Welsh were all but mathematically out of the World Cup.

Cocooned in the sardonic atmosphere of the press box, the main entertainment came once I'd spotted Mehmet across the stadium, wearing another extravagant suit. He watched about two minutes of the match and spent the rest, back to play, conducting the Turkish crowd with a mesmerising range of mannered and expansive sweeps of the arms.

Other than that, some Turkish pressure and a lucky Welsh draw.

'Don't look so gloomy,' said Neville Southall, gloomily. Minutes after a busy night in goal, Southall had been sent out to face the press. Gould may have been the coach but he refused to speak to them. Surrounded by empty cardboard boxes and practice cones, Southall, muddy kneed and sweaty, slept-walked through the conference. 'Giggs,' he said, 'is miles away from being the finished article.' Apparently the Welsh had 'tried to be a bit clever . . . not play the English game'.

7.00 p.m., 29 March 1997: Cardiff Arms Park

They were knocking the Arms Park down. The curving West Stand had had its seats ripped out and the cranes, carved against the acid blue sky, would be swinging their demolition balls within hours of the final whistle.

A press pass sat in my pocket, but for this game against

Belgium I had decided to sit with the crowd. Behind me were a pair of nasal Cardiff accents, to my mind's ear an unlovely sound, muddy, gravelly, not at all like the cartoon lilt of the Valleys. I was straining to hear their conversation, an informed analysis of Belgium teams past. 'What a great player Scifo was,' one was saying as the players lined up for the anthems.

Suddenly the Welsh players turned ninety degrees to face the deserted North Stand, the conductor raised his baton and I realised that my palms were slick with sweat.

A new sound behind me, no longer muddy or gravelly. Goose bumps I never knew I possessed – on the soles of my feet, across my eyeballs – sprang erect. Curious when written, curious when spoken, mellifluous when sung by a choir of Tenor-Gods like the ones behind me, is the Welsh language. The conductor had his body turned from the band to the crowd and was listening to them, conducting them, appreciating them.

This was the World Cup . . . Pity there were only 15,000 in here.

'Land of My Fathers' it translates as. Funny, that. It's as if the most beautiful thing the Welsh can do in the present (sing this inspiring, dolorous anthem) is to honour the nation's forefathers, its past.

The Belgians, two up by half time, were generations ahead of the Welsh. The visiting crowd were whooping it up, taunting the Welsh with derogatory, English, terrace chants.

'Fuck off you cunts,' yelled a Tenor-God.

'You're not singing any more,' sang the Belgians.

A Bass-God, his eyes popping, turned on his silent countrymen. 'Support your fucking country,' he screamed.

An exhortation that always begs the question (especially in Wales), 'Yes, but which country?' The country where only 50 per cent of people bothered to vote in a referendum for Welsh self-governance; and only 50 per cent of that 50 per cent wanted that independence? Or the country that speaks the language of the colonisers in the East and another language (its own) in the West? The country in which the North resents the South with its London-fawning 'Taffia' and the South mocks the North for being hicks? The country in which over 90 per cent of football fans support teams in the English Premiership? The country whose national team is managed by an Englishman?

'Support your fucking country.' Seats were being nervously vacated. Police had started to appear. I dug the press pass out of my pocket.

7.00 p.m. Saturday, 11 October 1997: Stade Roi Baudouin, Brussels

In the sparkling press box of what was once known as Heysel I dug into the free drink and started eyeing the televisions around the room.

'Excuse me?' I said to the Belgian press officer. 'When this game's over will these TVs have the second half of the England game on?'

'Maybe.'

Maybe?

The Italy–England game in Rome that evening had been the focus of attention all day.

'There'll be one hell of a party tonight if the Italians beat them,' Mark Evans, the Welsh FA press officer, had told me that morning in the Welsh team hotel.

'What game do you think they'll be watching on telly back in Cardiff?' I asked.

'Probably England.'

We didn't bother talking about the Wales game.

A plump Belgian kid was pacing nervously round the hotel foyer. Clutching a football, he was swamped in the red and white official merchandise of England's most famous club, desperate for a sight of Giggs. He didn't show. But Dean Saunders did! The kid pulled a face like he'd been made to eat every last bit of his mixed veg.

The Italy–England game was the focus of attention at the Stade Roi Baudouin as well. The man from the *Liverpool Post*, a Welshman, finally cracked when, after I had given him an earful about how good Hoddle's side was, I had one go too many at Gould. 'It's very easy to criticise,' he said, 'but you've got to give him some credit for travelling 30,000 miles a year and trying to learn Welsh.'

It had rained steadily all afternoon, and the stadium and crowd were blurred in the wet. The atmosphere was soggy too, the game devoid of any potential drama. As long as the Belgians beat the Welsh they were in the play-offs. Even if they lost, they were in the play-offs unless Turkey won in Holland. Trying to inject some urgency, the Welsh had talked about pride. Gould had masterminded the seventh worst defensive record in the European qualifying competition; better than only Azerbaijan, Liechtenstein, the Faeroe Islands, Malta, San Marino and Luxembourg. (And worse than Iceland, Armenia, Cyprus, Estonia and Slovenia, among others.) This game offered the chance to make a new start, plan for Euro 2000, blood youth . . .

One of those youths, Bristol City's Rob Edwards, then conceded a third-minute penalty. 1-0. Half an hour later, the keeper fumbled the ball. 2-0. Just before half time, a cross from the right. 3-0. Wales were in danger of slipping beneath Luxembourg in the defensive league table.

The second half started. Several hundred miles away, the first half was starting. 'Stand up if you hate England,' sang the hundred or so Welsh fans with gusto.

It was an extraordinary second half of terrible pathos thanks to Ryan Giggs, that 'unfinished article'. What a performance he gave. Earning a penalty and then tapping in a goal he had created from his own half, he almost got Wales a draw. It was as if his creaking sense of injustice at not going to France because he was Welsh finally cracked, leaving him with nothing to do but 'rage, rage against the dying of the light'. Incandescent with dark rage and untouchable. Shame it was all so irrelevant.

And there on the touchline was Gould, now quite mad. Drenched, his hair was flattened to his scalp and he was shouting indiscriminately at everyone in sight: officials, ball-boys (backing off nervously), the crowd, the police. As Giggs, fatuously, destroyed the Belgian defence once more, Gould launched into a bizarre series of dramatic poses – arms thrown wide; head on knees; crouching with torso and face twisted to the crowd, eyes like moons, an extended arm and finger pointing to the pitch. Stage laughter followed, arms on hips, chest puffed out, laughing first in the faces of FIFA officials and then, from two inches away, extraordinarily, rudely, in the face of Georges Leekens, the Belgian coach. Look at me, I picked Giggs, I picked the best player on the pitch, I did.

Which didn't stop them slipping out of the World Cup perfectly unnoticed while we all poured back into the dry where we had found *Rai Uno* on which to watch the second half of the match and I, my friend John, dozens of Belgian journalists and my Welsh colleague from the *Post* huddled round the screen and watched that most astonishing game of football as Ince bled, Wright hit the post, Vieri shaved the post and this is the World Cup.

the contributors

Patrick Barclay of the *Sunday Telegraph* has hardly ever written anything as long as his article for *Perfect Pitch*.

Hugo Borst. Dutch genius. Not fond of flying. Lives quietly with his wife and child.

Joe Boyle edits niche sports magazines. He works mainly in London, although he still pays his council tax in Cardiff.

Stuart Ford. An entertainment lawyer. Wore the England shirt a few times. Doesn't regret a thing.

Simon Inglis' first book, *The Football Grounds of Britain,* was chosen by Frank Keating as the best sports book of the century. Next century Simon will branch out of football grounds. But recently he wrote a centennial history of Villa Park.

Marcela Mora y Araujo, journalist, philosopher, follower of Noam Chomsky and former interpreter to Diego Maradona, is poised to become co-editor of *Perfect Pitch.*

Blake Morrison was once offered schoolboy forms by Preston North End. Had he accepted them, things might have been very different. But instead he wrote *And When Did You Last See Your Father?, As If,* and most recently, *Too True,* a collection of stories and essays, including one dealing with his failed football career and love for Burnley FC.

Frans Oosterwijk, minimalist with the Dutch weekly *Vrij Nederland*, is a star of the literary football magazine *Hard Gras*. And that's saying something. Doesn't know what a *doodshoofdvlinder* is in English.

Harry Ritchie grew up in Fife, where he went to school with Gordon Brown. He has written about British literature, British tourists on the Costa del Sol, and the last bits of the British Empire. The Scottish parliament could open up a whole new field.

Nicholas Royle writes novels and works for *Time Out*. He has also edited seven (seven!) anthologies of short stories.

D.J. Taylor is a novelist, critic and *Perfect Pitch* writer. Few people alive have read more books, and soon there will be no one who has written more. His novel *Trespass* appears in June, and his Thackeray biography next year.

Lynne Truss, novelist and *Times* columnist, may be an easy-to-please Johnny-come-lately when it comes to football, but she is also a critic by training. At the moment she is writing a novel called *Going Loco*. And *Tennyson's Gift* might be made into a film!

Simon Veksner is finishing his first novel, *Class A*, for the eighth time. As yet he has no plans to buy Manchester City and play himself at centre-forward. But he is a *Perfect Pitch* regular.

Luis Fernando Verissimo is a Brazilian newspaper columnist whose book *O analista de Bagé*, about a macho psychotherapist, has been reprinted 100 times.

perfect pitch

3) men and women

EDITED BY SIMON KUPER and MARCELA MORA Y ARAUJO

will be published on 3 September 1998 (ISBN 0 7472 7510 6) in Review softback, on a theme of men and women, and their relationship with football. Among those who will be writing for this third edition are:

Hugo Borst
Liz Crolley
Hunter Davies
Mark Fish
Simon Hughes
Simon Kuper
Emma Lindsey
Ian Macmillan
Julia Napier
Rob Newman
Joseph O'Connor
Amy Raphael
Harry Ritchie
Alyson Rudd

Further contributors will follow.

perfect pitch 4

will be published in spring 1999.